Copy right

Text Copyright © 2024 by Kirsten Morava

ISBN Paperback: 979-8-9890070-5-9
ISBN E-book: 979-8-9890070-6-6

Trigger warning

This book contains content that might be troubling for some readers. This includes, but is not limited to, adult content, sexual activities, various kinks and fetishes, rape, substance abuse, substance use, death, suicide, nightmares/night terrors, stalking, kidnapping, PTSD, multiple traumas, profanity, and so on.

Please take care of your mental health when reading Forever Angel.

Forever Angel

By

Kirsten Morava

Content

Chapter One
Scarlett and Noelle

Scarlett's eyes slowly opened into the dimly lit hospital room, where she became conscious of her surroundings—hearing all the machines that were pumping medicine into her daughter, Noelle. The night nurse was finishing her rounds, and none of the machines were setting off alarms. The last few days have been challenging. Noelle was not responding well, and her delicate five-year-old body was having a hard time fighting off the infection after this round.

Scarlett sat up and stretched to see her beautiful Noelle sleeping peacefully. Every fiber in her body hated seeing her precious baby fighting for her life. If she could have one wish as a mother, it would be to be the one dealing with this, not her. Scarlett doesn't dare to cry in front of her. Noelle needs to know that her mom is strong. No matter the stress, they can handle whatever is thrown at them. They are a team when it comes to fighting.

Although Scarlett puts on a perfect mom poker face, her mind drifts amidst the chaos of doctors, treatments, and uncertainty. The determination Scarlett feels as a mother to prove to Noelle that she would never give up on her, like her father did when he found out that she had cancer. His absence felt like betrayal. How could he abandon them in their darkest hour? It was a struggle to comprehend how someone could walk away when their child needed them the most, leaving a mother to be single to bear the weight of fear and despair alone. Watching Noelle stir in the hospital, she concluded that Scarlett would fight with or without him by her side.

"Good morning, Scarlett. Everything is looking swell," said nurse Cali. I squeezed her hand in reassurance, *"Good morning, Cali, hopefully we stay uphill."* Scarlett whispered. Scarlett quietly went into the bathroom to freshen up, washing her face with cold water to wake herself up and reduce the puffiness around her eyes, thereby hiding any indication that she was crying. Staring into the mirror, Scarlett took a deep breath before leaving the bathroom and embracing the day. Scarlett took one more look at Noelle, who was peacefully

sleeping. A soft smile crossed her face as she quickly went over to the coffee station to get some much-needed caffeine.

Once back inside the room, Scarlett sat in silence as she answered emails for work. The last couple of days have been rough. Between being a present mother, understanding medical terminology, and of course answering the editor. Scarlett felt stuck, especially since everything was at a standstill for Noelle. It is not fair to be stuck in the middle, keeping a job and caring for Noelle. For once, can someone care for me? Scarlett thought to herself as she fought back disappointment. Scarlett quickly started typing away to finish the chapter that was due. Suddenly, she saw Noelle collapse and start seizing. Scarlett's motherly instincts kicked in. Her focus swiftly shifted from work to tending to her daughter. With trembling hands, she cried out for help, Scarlett's heart pounding with fear as she witnessed Noelle collapsing into a seizure.

In that moment, time stood still, as panic engulfed the hospital room. Amidst the chaos of the room being transformed into a whirlwind of urgency as the medical team rushed in, their steps echoed with purpose. Each passing second was a mix of fear and determination to stabilize Noelle.

A couple of hours later, Noelle started to stir as she woke up. Scarlett was finishing the email containing the chapter that needed to be sent to the editor. As I closed the laptop and walked over to greet Noelle, the oncologist came in.

"Good morning, Noelle, how are we feeling today?" asked Dr. Smith. Struggling to sit up in the gurney, Noelle replies, "Hungry, can I go home, *Dr. Smith?"* Dr. Smith smiled while grabbing the stethoscope to listen to Noelle's lungs. *"Hungry is a good sign, hopefully soon, but we still need to watch you to make sure you are recovering well."* Dr. Smith said, while Noelle just stared at her mom with sad eyes. Scarlette whispered, *"I will get you a donut today."* Noelle smiled, and they both winked at each other. *"A donut? Lucky!"* Dr. Smith chuckled as he updated Noelle's chart.

Just a few minutes later, there was a knock at the door. *"How is my sweet fighter?"* A soothing, familiar voice grabs our attention as a smile beamed radiantly from Noelle when she shouts, ***"GRANDMA!!!** You came just in time for mommy to get donuts! Can you stay with me?"* We smiled at each other as she traded off shifts on watching Noelle.

As I made my way to the parking lot, I was stopped by the case manager, who pulled me aside to tell me that she had put our information in for the Angel Tree. Gratitude filled my heart that she was able to get us on it at the last minute.

This round of bills is going to kick my ass. We are already struggling, but knowing we could get adopted could help us out a lot. Depending on the cost we are facing, we will probably be facing eviction, which breaks my heart. I will be damned to let Noelle know that.

My phone rang as I walked into the shopping center, where I was trying to find the donut shop. It was Claire, *"Hello Claire, what is going on?"* Scarlett answered. *"As your best friend and honorary Godmother of my baby*

Noelle, I need to know how she is doing since I am stuck at work and cannot make it until later this evening," Claire said. I smiled at her response, "Noelle is doing better, still going to be a couple of days. *I am on the way to the bakery to get a donut to cheer her up. Oh, and we got on the angel tree!"* Scarlett said with excitement. Claire squeaked in excitement about the news.

Little did Scarlett know that a few steps away was a listening ear from an inquisitive mind. She was so engrossed in chatting with her friend on the phone that Nikolas forgot what he was looking for. He followed her to the bakery, listening intently as she shared one side of the story. She explained that her daughter, Noelle, had a special wish for Christmas, and this year's Celebration was especially meaningful because Noelle was recovering from her infection. Nikolas pulled out his phone and was jotting down all the information he was hearing from Scarlett. He snapped a couple of photos for safekeeping.

Scarlett hung up the phone and went into the bakery. Nikolas followed her in. Scarlett has already pulled on the heartstrings of Nikolas. He interrupted the cashier and flashed a dashing smile to Scarlett, "Let me treat you today, beautiful. It *is the holiday season to pay it forward."* Nikolas said charmingly. Scarlett was blushing at this gentleman. *"Thank you, I really appreciate it."* Nikolas smiled, *"It is an honor, Miss*?" He said with a questioning tone. *"Scarlett,"* Scarlett said in a nervous tone. Nikolas stared admiringly into Scarlett's green eyes. *"A beautiful name for a beautiful woman."* They both smiled and walked out of the bakery together, making small talk. When the cool December air hit their faces, Scarlett shivered, and her flushed colored cheeks cooled down to turn white. She was in a not-so-warm jacket; Nikolas took his scarf and wrapped it around Scarlett. Of course, she insisted she wasn't a bother to him, but he insisted she take it.

They split ways, and Scarlett could not help but smile from ear to ear. She felt warmer with Nikolas's scarf and continued daydreaming about the charming stranger. She could smell his cologne on the scarf, and on the way back to the hospital, Scarlett could not help but hold the scarf close to her nose as she smelled it.

Walking back into the room, Scarlett saw Noelle throwing up, and she rushed in to be by her daughter's side and help her clean up. *"Did you just get your morning round of medicine?"* Scarlett asked. Noelle, wiping the tears away from her eyes, says, "Yeah, I really hate them,*"* sniffling. Grandma interrupts, "Here is a wet washcloth, *dear, and a new pail for you if you get sick again. You are a strong little one, and it won't be like this forever. You are a fighter."* They all smiled warmly at each other when Grandma noticed the scarf around Scarlett's neck. *"Where did you get that scarf, Scarlett*?" Grandma asked. In an embarrassed tone, "Oh, *this, I had it in the car for a while."* Grandma looked at Scarlett, knowing better, but she understood that Scarlett didn't want to bring it up around Noelle. They all sat around, enjoying their donuts and some cartoons, before it was time to run some more tests.

Throughout the day, nurses and doctors came to check on Noelle, with every poke of a needle to draw blood, every medicine insert, or fluid bag to get switched out. Scarlett stopped working and came to be beside Noelle. With sadness in her eyes, Scarlett's heart broke as she realized her daughter just wanted to go home and be a normal child. When the medical staff left, there were tears of sadness and cuddles. Noelle fell asleep soundly in Grandma's arms.

Later that evening, Claire came by and surprised the family with dinner from Noelle's favorite burger place, and an even more special surprise: Noelle got a new stuffed animal and coloring book from her Godmother. Seeing her smile was worth everything. As everyone chatted, Scarlett noticed Noelle was struggling to keep her eyes open. She walked over, tucked in Noelle, and kissed her, letting her know it was ok to go to sleep. Clair and Grandma headed out, and Scarlett set her chair up to do some much-needed work. She looked over to see the scarf in her bag. A subtle smile crossed her full lips as she reminisced about her short time with Nikolas.

Scarlett pondered to herself if she would ever see that man again. Walking over to the scarf. She danced it along in her hands, focusing on the texture of each fiber as she stared lovingly at it. Wrapping it around her arm as she brings it close to her chest in a warm embrace, and taking a deep breath to inhale the aroma of the first man

who was able to make her smile in a long time.

Chapter two
Nikolas

Nikolas was a wealthy, stunning man in his mid-forties, standing six feet four inches tall. He took care of his body with a delicious six-pack, clean-cut black hair, radiant smile, and gorgeous tan. As part of his daily routine, he normally scavenges for his angels around this time. He went from store to store, trying to find the next single mom to take care of.

He was pretty good at finding the single moms on the list. He saw it as his charity work with a twist. Nikolas sought to fulfill his desire during the season of giving by supporting single moms with their bills in January, ensuring the kids received exactly what they wanted and needed for the holiday season. But he was going to get something in return. Nikolas was a man of wants and desires. His goal was to see how many moms he could spoil and stuff their stockings.

Scarlett caught his attention while he was stalking the moms; he already had angel cards for them. At the same time, she was on the phone ahead of him. He listened to the conversation and gathered a wealth of information about his new prey. He enjoyed how Scarlett looked, her slim figure, long brown hair, green eyes, and full lips.

He wanted to see her dressed up as a present and ready to take him on her knees. After their small encounter, Nikolas went on a hunt to find her Angel Tree card. Roughly five stores around town, he was able to see it. He put the Angel Card in the pocket of his coat for safekeeping.

After finding it, he decided to walk around and do shopping for the stack of angel cards he had. Meticulously planning an accidental bump into one of his angels over by the dairy section. As she backed up from reaching into the cooler to get a gallon of milk for her kids, she accidentally bumped into Nikolas. She turned around, and her mouth dropped when she saw this gorgeous giant. *"I am so sorry, sir!"* she said. He looked at her with a charming look. *"It is perfectly fine; you can bump into me any time."* They stood there for a couple of minutes talking, and just before leaving, they parted ways. Nikolas invited his Angel out for dinner. She was stunned that someone of Nikolas's looks asked her out to dinner. She agreed to meet for dinner that evening.

A couple of hours into the dinner, they were hitting it off. Nikolas was pouring the sultry charm on his Angel. Oblivious to his actions, she wrapped around him at dinner. Nikolas leaned in and kissed her before whispering into her ear, *"I would love to have you over at my place, you're an angel and deserve to be worshiped."* Upon hearing this, she asked while biting her bottom lip seductively, *"How quickly can we get to your place?"* He quickly paid for dinner, and they bolted out the door back to his place.

Barely getting inside his home, they started to ravish each other, passionately crashing their lips upon each other as their hands viciously stripped off each layer of their clothes.

Nikolas guided his angel to his extra-large couch and pushed her down to lie there as he admired her body in green crotchless lingerie. Nikolas then crawls up to his desert for the night. He admires seeing her pink lips.

Hooking his arms around her waist, he pulls her down to his face and eats her treat like a hungry animal. Tongue fucking her as her back arches in pleasure, his tongue dances around her clit, making it swell larger and larger.

As he sucks her clit harder, he shoves two fingers in fucking her nice and slow. His angel's moans turn into pleasurable screams as he finger fucks her faster. Finally, she came in his mouth. Nikolas' aching cock couldn't take it anymore. He pulls himself up as he leaves a trail of kisses, worshiping his angel all the way up to her neck, burying his cock deep into her tight, forgotten pussy.

They matched their thrust to each other, going harder and harder. His angel got on top and worshiped Nikolas, twisting her hips up and down on his engorged cock. Bouncing harder and harder as he grabbed her tits to suck on. His angel leaned her head back and started to squirt all over Nikolas as she felt him explode inside her, cum mixing. She collapsed onto his chest as they tried to catch their breath.

As the night ended, Nikolas took his Angel back to her home. After arriving, Nikolas pulled out his checkbook, saying, *"An angel so magnificent as you shall not struggle but be worshiped on all levels. If I don't get to see you before Christmas, here is my gift to you."* He slips her a check as she stares at him with a blank look on her face. While accepting the check for $10,000, she stuttered, *"I...I can't accept this."* Nikolas replied, *"You will, my angel."* A tear rolled down her face. *"Thank you."* He watched his angel walk into her apartment before taking off.

Once the door shut from tonight's angel apartment, Nikolas walked back to his car, the soft, crunchy gravel under his feet barely registered as his mind wandered elsewhere. Thoughts of Scarlett began to fill his head. He wanted to know more about the woman from the bakery. Nikolas could not shake the thoughts of Scarlett. The temptation of knowing her is an itch he can't get rid of.

Once he got home, he grabbed a nightcap of whiskey and went straight to his office to research the mysterious woman named Scarlett. He had to get his hands on her. He jotted down all the information he heard on the phone conversation she had, searching for her name. He found that she was a writer, an advocate for children who are battling cancer, and had a piece of shit husband who abandoned her when Noelle was first diagnosed with cancer.

Hours have passed while he dives deeper into his research, learning everything possible about Scarlett. The more he knew about her, the more he became obsessed with her. She was a literal angel. Nikolas wanted to do more than worship her. He wanted her. He had to figure out a game plan on how to keep bumping into her. Nikolas cleared his schedule for tomorrow. He wanted to stand guard at the hospital to observe her daily routine and plan his next move on Scarlett.

Chapter three
Stand by

    Morning came, and Nikolas had very little rest as he was up researching Scarlett most of the night. As he made his coffee, all he could think about was her being tied up like a present with a large bow draped delicately over her perfectly round ass. He packed his belongings and started to make his way to the hospital closest to the bakery, where he bumped into Scarlett.

Back at the hospital, Scarlett was slowly waking up after a rough night with Noelle. Just as they thought she was getting better, Noelle's condition quickly took a turn for the worse. Tears-soaked Scarlett's face as she cried quietly into the sleeve of her hoodie, praying that her daughter would pull through.

Nikolas pulled up and decided to head into the hospital to see if he could find more information. Walking past the double sliding doors to the sweetest elderly woman working the information desk. Nikolas put on his charm and dazzling smile. *"Can you point me in the direction of the pediatric oncology floor?"* The woman at the information desk answered, *"Yes, go to the elevator right over there and take it up to floor 3."* Nikolas thanked her and squeezed her hand as he headed towards the elevators.

As the elevator climbed each floor, he was getting excited to lay his eyes on Scarlett again. When the doors slid open, he stepped out and walked the halls cautiously so as not to be seen. The staff was busy doing their morning rounds. Nikolas quickly hid behind a corner as if he were answering a message on his phone when Scarlett came out of the room to grab some coffee.

He didn't want to be spotted by her, but he marked down the room number they were in and snapped a quick photo of a map. Nikolas started to head back to his car to wait for Scarlett's next move to see if she leaves. Nikolas overheard the staff discussing how Santa was going to visit the kids next week.

That's when the brilliant idea of him being Santa came to mind. What better way to spend more time with Scarlett than to play Santa at the hospital? Alarms started going off, and the medical staff and Scarlett rushed to Noelle's room to take care of her. Now was the time for Nikolas to make his escape when no one would see him leaving. This was Nikolas' chance to escape back to his car without anyone seeing him. He thanked the woman at the information desk again and said a quick prayer that Noelle would get better immediately.

Scarlett rushed to her daughter as her heart was pounding out of her chest, and her hand was covered in the hot coffee she spilled. Noelle was violently throwing up to the point she was not able to catch her breath, which triggered her oxygen level to drop significantly. The nurses quickly administered nausea medication through Noelle's IV and put her on oxygen to help build her lung strength back up. Another nurse was aiding Scarlett's burns from her coffee.

Nikolas was worried about Noelle and Scarlett. He consulted the online map of the hospital and determined the room number. He drove his Genesis around the hospital and parked in perfect view of Noelle's room. Roughly 30 minutes have passed by, and he notices windows being opened in Noelle's room. He saw Scarlett, and pain hit his soul when he noticed her hand was bandaged up.

Nikolas pondered to himself that she must have spilled coffee all over herself when the alarms went off. The thought of Scarlett being hurt upset Nikolas as Scarlett stood at the window, staring off into town. Nikolas watched Scarlett from his car Noelle must have been asleep because Scarlett took Nikolas's scarf to comfort her.

She ran her fingers along the scarf, feeling the softness. Holding it close to her face, she inhales the aroma of the scarf, her head tilted to the side as she embraces the scarf in a tight hug. Nikolas smiled as he watched her comfort herself with his scarf. It filled his heart with joy knowing he could be her peace.

Nikolas sat back in his seat after watching Scarlett comfort herself. He took a deep breath before promising himself that he would never let Scarlett be disappointed in a man ever again and that he would make you his forever angel.

Around lunchtime, Scarlett was on the move. Nikolas carefully followed her drive towards the restaurant, keeping his distance as she walked in to place her order. He covered up with a baseball hat and a hoodie. Keeping a couple of feet back, he listened to her order. Nikolas had to fight with every fiber in his body not to pay for her meal. He had to sit back and study her every move.

Once Scarlett got her order, she was on the move again; her next stop was a quick drive-through for coffee. She ordered three drinks: a children's hot chocolate, a hot white mocha, and a refreshing passion fruit green tea spritz. Nikolas made sure to get the same order. He was becoming obsessed with Scarlett. Anything that her mouth tasted, he had to taste as well.

The evening rolled around, and Nikolas felt the urge to go back into the hospital again to sneak closer to Noelle's room. He reached into the go bag and grabbed his travel-size bottle of the same cologne. He wanted to freshen up his scarf for Scarlett. Nikolas carefully slipped past the sliding glass doors and confidently made his way to the elevators to go to the third floor. The feeling of possibly running into Scarlett gave Nikolas a high that was hard to explain.

Cautiously walking the halls, Nikolas walked right by Noelle's room. The schedule board stated that she was undergoing chemotherapy. Nikolas stepped inside and examined the room. It was a tiny apartment with toys around for Noelle and Scarlett's laptop. Nikolas walked over to see the computer, only to find it locked. However, in the bag, he noticed his scarf. Quickly, he pulled his cologne out and spritzed a couple of sprays to make sure Scarlett could smell him for a few more days.

Nikolas escaped the room like a thief in the night before being noticed. He made sure to snap a couple of photos for safekeeping, adding to his research. On the way out, his phone alerted him that it was time to visit his next

angel on the list.

Chapter four
Angels

The morning sun rose as Nikolas lay there in his satin sheets, stretching. The sun rays dance upon every inch of his bare torso, warming the hairs on his happy trail. It was another day to do Santa's work. More angels needed attention and pleasure. But Nikolas's urges towards Scarlett were growing stronger. Nikolas missed Scarlett's infectious smile and her sweet aroma.

The desire to see Scarlett was becoming like a drug. Nikolas had to lay his eyes on her before attending to his other angels. Before his shopping spree, he quickly made his way to the hospital to see if he could get a glimpse of Scarlett. When he arrived at the hospital, he found his favorite parking spot. The one that looks directly up to Noelle's hospital room. He sees the back of someone's head in her room. They are wearing a knitted beanie with the lights completely dimmed, making it challenging to see who it was. Nikolas' fingers started to tingle as he battled with his thoughts and urges. Should he go in or should he leave? It was a tug-of-war within his thoughts. The tingling sensation below his belt was winning. Nikolas's urges became overpowering as he turned off the car and headed inside the hospital.

Nikolas made his way up to Noelle's room nonchalantly, but the door was shut. Casually stepping closer to the door and pulling out his phone to look inconspicuous, he listened to the conversation behind the door. It was muffled, but he could hear a man's voice and Scarlett talking; it was hard to listen to what exactly was going on behind the door. Anger began to fill his veins as if there was another prospector in Scarlett's life. Nikolas was determined now more than ever to make Scarlett his.

Nikolas' phone once again alerted him that it was almost time to get the shopping done and meet with his angels. His fury drove his addiction even more. None of his angels will be able to walk by the end of tonight. As he got into the elevator, the mysterious man with Scarlett left. Nikolas checked his notes and started to make his way to the outlets to run into the Angel that he was going to rip to shreds this morning.

Pulling into the parking lot, he spots his target. Thinking of the game plan to grab her attention, he parks next to her, almost colliding with her as he goes to grab something as she is heading into the driver's seat. Startled, the angel says, "Oh, *I am so sorry.*" Nikolas holds onto her hips to stabilize her from falling over. A devilish grin crosses his lips. "*An Angel as beautiful as you doesn't need to apologize.*" He could feel her quiver under his grip. Her smile turns into a bite on her bottom lip. "*You are so kind and handsome.*" She speaks. "*You should let me spoil you this morning for getting in your way,*" Nikolas says in a low growl. A nervous giggle escaped her mouth as she locked the car and followed his lead.

Store to store, they went and purchased everything the angel desired. With each favor she requested from Nikolas, the more handsy he became. By the third store, they were exchanging steamy kisses. Walking around, he found a pair of sexy pink lingerie. In Nikolas' mind, it would be breathtakingly beautiful on Scarlett as he became hard, thinking about pulling it off with his teeth. But those thoughts became interrupted as his morning time angel snatched it from his hand and whispered, *"Follow me."*

She led him into the dressing room and made him sit down in the chair. She began slowly stripping down for him and put the pink lingerie on as she showed off her body. Moving her fingernails along her skin while dancing for Nikolas. She stepped forward and leaned down, placing her hands on Nikolas's knees as she bent down and unzipped his pants. Pulling his stiff cock out, she wanted to show her appreciation.

On her knees, Nikolas' morning Angel leaned in and licked the base of his cock, slowly massaging him all to the tip. He engulfed his thick cock deep into her mouth as she massaged him up and down. He entangled his fingers in her long brown hair, helping her bob her head up and down. Nikolas' eyes roll to the back of his head as he enjoys the gentle sensation. He rolls his head back up to watch her beautiful mouth swallow him.

A grin came across his face. His grip tightened in her hair as he started to buck his hips into her mouth. Pumping harder and faster as she gags. Tears streamed down her face. Nikolas stands up while holding his Angel's head as he pounds her throat. Their eyes lock as he explodes deep down into her throat, making her swallow all his juices.

Panting and out of breath, Nikolas fixes himself and rips the price tag off the lingerie to pay for it as the Angel fixes herself in the dressing room. Frustrated with himself, all Nikolas could think about was seeing Scarlett in the lingerie. He paid and left the Angel he treated behind with no trace of ever contacting them again.

Nikolas quickly got into his car and sped off. He was determined to get to the one Angel he truly wanted. Scarlett.

Chapter five
Surprise

Grandma was settling in at the hospital to spend a couple of hours with Noelle. Scarlett had a friend in town whom she hadn't seen in several years. Although Scarlett wanted to stay with her daughter, she knew it would be a long time before she saw her friend again. Breaks were particularly beneficial for a burnt-out single mother. Although guilt swarmed throughout Scarlett's mind, she had to keep reminding herself that it was ok to go out for dinner with a friend she had not seen in years. Noelle was safe and ok in the hospital and with her grandma.

Gathering her purse and giving Noelle a bunch of love before leaving, she made her way down to the parking lot, entering her car. Scarlett had an eerie feeling that someone was watching her. She brushed it off. Maybe it was mixed signals from the guilt of leaving Noelle's side. Her feeling was not wrong, though. A few cars down, there sat Nikolas, waiting for his forever angel, Scarlett.

He pondered her plans and the reasons behind her being caught in a mental tug of war. He waited to leave as she drove off. He swiped open his phone and pulled up the tracking app. Nikolas took a deep breath and followed Scarlett at a safe distance until they reached the restaurant. He stayed in his car watching Scarlett as she waited outside. A woman approached her, and her smile could light up the night sky. They exchanged hugs and made their way inside.

Nikolas quietly made his way inside the restaurant and took a seat near them at the bar just in earshot of the two girlfriends gossiping. Although his back was to them, he listened in as they laughed, shared memories of the past, and talked about the now. He felt joyous learning so much about Scarlett and hearing her voice light up as she released stress. Scarlett sounded like a brand-new woman.

The eerie feeling of being watched kept churning inside Scarlett's stomach. With every sip of her cocktail, she tried her hardest to ignore it. She excused herself to the bathroom. Nikolas waited a minute and hung out in the hallway before accidentally bumping into Scarlett. He had to touch her and smell her sweet aroma.

Scarlett walked out of the bathroom with her head down, looking at her phone, as she collided with Nikolas in the hallway. He embraced her in his arms and spun her around, pinning her to the wall to keep her from losing balance. He kept his head down at an angle, staring at her luscious lips as he apologized for running into her. She softly panted an apology to Nikolas. Nikolas fought with every fiber of his being not to lock his lips with hers.

Awkwardness grew as they stared deep into each other's eyes. Nikolas could feel his cock start to harden as he was pressed up against Scarlett. Nervously, he rushed into the bathroom and brought Scarlett back to her friend. Nikolas leaned against the bathroom wall as he tried to calm his cock down. Battling with the thoughts in his head, the main idea was *"Scarlett will be an addiction I cannot break."*

Back at the booth, Scarlett was having a battle within herself. Between her many thoughts of *"I should have kissed him"* and "he is a stranger," but "he looked so familiar," she had a hard time focusing on the conversation with her friend. Scarlett kept casually looking around to see if she could spot the mysterious man she had almost fucked in the hallway. But he was nowhere to be seen.

Nikolas quietly made his way to Scarlett's server and paid for the dinner bill. When it was time for Scarlett and her friend to pay the bill, the server mentioned that it was taken care of. Confusion crossed Scarlett's and her friend's faces, but Scarlett had an idea of what had happened.

Nikolas waited in his car in perfect view of Scarlett's car. He sits there waiting as she gets inside. The way the parking lot lights illuminated her features, Nikolas could not help but play with his cock while following her back to the hospital. Jerking himself as his memories flash back to them being pinned together in the hallway. The urge to pick her up and fuck her right there in the hallway makes him explode as he arrives in the hospital parking lot moments after Scarlett heads back upstairs to Noelle.

Back upstairs, Scarlett quickly embraces Noelle in a hug, and the guilt of leaving her for a couple of hours disappears. As she catches up with her daughter and her mom, she feels revived after the brief respite she was given. The eerie feeling of being watched calms down as she cozies up in her spot near the window. Down below, hidden in the shadows, Nikolas leans back in the car, watching his precious forever angel.

Scarlett could not rest. She tossed and turned all night, sporadically peeping out the window. Maybe it was all in her head; the eerie feeling of being watched had to be paranoia arising from stress. Looking out of the window, she was able to see the moon in its full glory. Scarlett repeats a prayer, "Please, let everyone I love be safe, let the worries slip away, the stress disperses from my exhausted soul as we wake tomorrow for another day," she whispered.

In the parking lot, Nikolas looks up and wonders what Scarlett is saying as she admires the moon.

Chapter Six
Santa

Morning arrives, and patients and hospital staff begin to stir. Nikolas' curiosity is getting the best of him as he decides to walk the halls of the hospital stealthily. Listening to the chatter among the healthcare staff. *"Santa is coming."* One nurse says. *"That will be exciting for the children."* Another one replies. The gears in Nikolas's head were turning as he listened to the conversations. Nikolas's urge to know who was going to be playing the role of Santa had become his goal today. As they followed the nurses, they chatted about their night and expressed their hope for the floor to be fully staffed. Nikolas rolled his eyes, growing agitated as he wanted them to discuss who would be Santa.

He noticed a group of nurses discussing Santa's Day and decided to follow them discreetly. *"Who is going to play Santa?"* someone in the group asked. *"I'm sure it will be Christopher from marketing, he has done it the last couple of years, from my understanding,"* another one mentioned.

An accomplished smile formed from the corners of Nikolas' lips as he turned the corner to think of the game plan to find Christopher. Nikolas made his way towards the elevator. As he was waiting to get on, he came to a halt when the elevator doors swung open, and out came Scarlett holding a cup of coffee. His head ducked down and quietly snuck in as she was leaving.

Nikolas leaned against the elevator walls and let out a sigh of relief as his cover was almost blown. Down several hallways, Nikolas found himself in the administration hallway. Door to door, Nikolas looked for the Marketing Manager. After a couple of turns, he finally found Christopher's door wide open as he was working on his computer. Nikolas respectfully knocked on Christopher's door.

"Good morning, Mr. Christopher. My name is Nikolas, and one of the lovely staff members here told me you are the person in charge of Santa's visit. I was curious if you needed any help, as I would love to volunteer."

Christopher greeted Nikolas, "Come in, I am the one who *usually plays Santa. But it seems like Santa heard my case and sent you to me. I have something personal happening and needed a volunteer."* Nikolas smiled in achievement as the two chatted about the details. An hour passed by, and Nikolas gathered all the necessary information for Santa Day.

Nikolas practiced for the next couple of days, studying Christmas movies to prepare for his role. He pondered what clues he could give Scarlett to let her know it was him. Before the night ended, the doorbell rang. It was his grocery delivery of candy canes and little teddy bears to hand to the kids after each visit. He grabbed a velvet bag to put the goodies in.

The big day arrived; Nikolas woke up feeling jollier than ever before. He knew he was ready to play the role of cheering up the children, and hopefully, have Scarlett sit on his lap. He just needed to make sure Noelle's room was the last room he visited. He approached Christopher's office to get into character before heading to the pediatric floor.

Making a mental note of where to start and stop as soon as he reached the floor, Noelle's room would be the last. So far, Nikolas' plan is working smoothly. Room to room, Nikolas played his role perfectly, laughing and jiggling like a bowl full of jelly, and bringing infectious smiles to all the kids. Meanwhile, family members hid their tears of happiness as they saw their babies enjoy their *"normal"* day.

Some moms hadn't been touched in a while, but their touch lingered, and their flirtatious comments were loud and clear. They wanted to scream for Father Christmas to take them and fill their stockings with presents. With how tempting it would be to bend the needy moms over and make them the perfect little Santa's helpers, Nikolas had to stay focused. The end goal is Scarlett!

A couple of hours passed, and it was Noelle's turn—my last room. I can take my time and maybe get Scarlett to sit on my lap to feel my yule log that wants to turn her into pound cake. The thought of her wiggling on my lap turned me on more and more.

*"**HO, HO, HO,**"* Nikolas joyfully belted as he entered Noelle's room. Noelle and Scarlett's faces lit up with happiness and joy as their time with Santa was finally here. Nikolas pulled up a chair next to Noelle's bed. Noelle shared her artwork, discussed her dreams and ambitions, and revealed what she wanted to do once she was healthy again. Scarlett sat back and watched her daughter and Santa talk like they were best of friends. Scarlett snapped a couple of photos of the two of them during his visit. Noelle's energy was quickly draining, and she started to drift off to sleep. Scarlett walked up and touched Nikolas' shoulder gently. "I apologize, she gets these bursts of energy and just as fast as it comes, *it leaves.*" Nikolas reached over and held her hand and strummed his thumb over her skin. "Heroes *never apologize. She is remarkable just like her mother.*" Scarlett smiled softly as she stared into Santa's dreamy eyes, getting lost in the moment. Nikolas smiled, *"Come sit on Santa's lap and tell me what you would like for Christmas."* Nikolas chuckled as he patted his lap. Scarlett laughed and took him up on his offer. Nikolas thought to himself, *"My planned work, I hope she craves my huge*

log." A smile crossed his lips as he leaned in to smell Scarlett's aroma as she nestled herself into his lap.

They talked for several minutes, and sporadically, he would adjust his lap to tease Scarlett. His hand started to softly rub her low back as he sneakily sniffed Scarlett's hair. Scarlett got a whiff of Nikolas' cologne; she froze for a minute as his scent lingered, trying to capture a memory for Scarlett. She recognizes that familiar smell, but can't quite place where it is. Nikolas had a gut feeling that she was onto him, so he swiftly adjusted his lap to distract her.

Scarlett could feel his growing member, but she felt so naughty with this attractive stranger. The urge to kiss him was starting to become overpowering. Innocently, she twisted her hips on his lap, which made a groan escape Nikolas' mouth. Nikolas leaned over Scarlett's neck and tickled her with the beard. Hearing his groan started to make Scarlett moist. She had to fight the urge to take Santa into the bathroom to jingle his bells.

Scarlett jumped up and shook the thought of getting dirty with Santa out of her head. But Nikolas' present was clearly making its presence known. Nikolas took a minute before standing up. His thoughts of making Scarlett his were just as strong as Scarlett's thoughts of jingling Santa's bells. They walked to the door, and just as Santa was about to leave, Nikolas leaned in and pulled Scarlett into his embrace, and kissed her passionately in the hallway. Her arms wrapped around Nikolas' neck. Scarlett snapped out of the crazy desire of fucking Santa when she heard Noelle's monitor. Noelle briefly woke up, thinking she must have been in a dream, as she saw her mom kissing Santa.

Chapter Seven

Gut Feeling

Scarlett could not shake the lasting impression of the steamy kiss she shared with Santa, let alone the tingling sensation between her legs. She regrets not finding out who he was. It has been a long time since Scarlett has allowed a man to take care of her. Scarlett was craving more of Santa's touch. It was starting to drive her mad. Scarlett turned on the water and tried to wash her hungry skin. The thoughts of who that man was and how she could find him danced in her head most of that night.

Nikolas did the final check-in before leaving for the parking lot, where he sat in his spot watching Scarlett stare off into the moon. He was desperate to know what she was feeling and thinking. Nikolas' throbbing cock ached for Scarlett. He was disappointed in himself; he could have had his Scarlett right there. Both were starving for each other's touch.

Nikolas devised a plan to follow Scarlett until he could get her alone. His aching balls started to hurt more from needing a release. As he stared at her beautiful features in the moonlight, Nikolas grabbed a hoodie from the back seat and unzipped his pants. Nikolas' hand danced up and down his throbbing cock as he gazed up at Scarlett. If only she knew what she did to me. Slowly jerking himself, imagining he was inside Scarlett with her pinned against the wall, moaning in his ear. His eyes rolled to the back of his head as he exploded all over his hoodie.

Morning came, and Scarlett had to get errands done while Grandma stayed with Noelle. When she made her way to the car, she was oblivious that Nikolas was already on the prowl. Then again, who could blame her? She spent the entire night pondering who was behind the beard and what she wanted to do to him. If she had the chance to meet him again, she knew she would rock his world without any hesitation.

After a couple of places, Scarlett started to feel uneasy. Not the kind of feeling that's sick, but a different kind of uneasiness. Nikolas was hot on her trail, and by the body language Scarlett was giving, he knew he had to back off. Nikolas battled with his urges and stepped outside to wait for Scarlett to come out of the store. When she came out, she headed down the road to a multilevel building.

Nikolas let her get several feet ahead before following her trail. But the uneasiness of someone following Scarlett began to intensify. She started to watch over her shoulder, which was becoming challenging for Nikolas as he tried to hide behind several people every few feet. When Scarlett finally did a complete turn around because her gut instinct was screaming at her, Nikolas quickly ducked into a building to hide from Scarlett.

He kept himself busy in the store while Scarlett ended her errands, fearing she was being followed, and then headed back to the hospital. Nikolas strolled around the store, keeping an eye out for Scarlett through the window. When she quickly passed by, Nikolas rushed out to catch up with her, but lost her in a group setting. Scarlett's uneasiness became gut-wrenching. She didn't want to make it obvious, but she rushed back to the hospital, where it was safe, back with Noelle.

Nikolas was frustrated that he had lost Scarlett in the group. He needed to get his fix; Scarlett was his kryptonite. Nikolas growled under his breath in defeat. Scarlett was nowhere to be found. He knew she was heading towards the multilevel building, but he left when she got an eerie feeling. Nikolas made his way to the building to see what the directory was for.

There were a couple of things that caught Nikolas' eye. Among the few shopping stores and doctor offices, one that stood out the most on the fifth floor was a support group. Nikolas quickly jotted down the places that Scarlett could go to before heading up to the fifth floor to get more information on the support group. Nikolas put on the charm with the front desk to get a flyer to see if there was one Scarlett would more than likely go to. The flyer read:

Welcome to Support Haven—a safe place to be heard and seen. Everyone is welcome.

Monday – Substance Sobriety
Tuesday – Cancer Battle
Wednesday – Winning Grief
Thursday – Parents' Day
Friday – Veterans

Scarlett would go there for Cancer Battle or Parents' Day. What better way to cope than with others who know about life themselves? Nikolas saved the details in his phone, hoping to catch her at one of the meetings.

Back at the hospital, Scarlett took a deep breath before going back into mom mode and being present for Noelle. It had been a rough morning for Noelle, as her body was feeling weak with the treatments. Scarlett shook off her uneasiness, knowing Noelle was not good. Mother's intuition, she felt guilty for leaving her sick child. Once Scarlett came back to the hospital and laid eyes on Noelle, the uneasiness disappeared.

As evening fell, the uneasiness returned. Scarlett was confused about the sensation she was feeling. She was with Noelle. Why did she feel this way? Little did she know Nikolas was gazing up from the car, waiting to see moonlight dance upon Scarlett's face.

Chapter Eight
Pinned

Several days have passed, and although it has been brutally exhausting with a sick child. It was time for Scarlett to take care of her mental health, since she is now dealing with everything alone. It was Cancer Battle Day at Support Haven, where the support group gathered. Scarlett wanted to meet other parents who were the backbone of their child. Scarlett hated leaving Noelle behind at the hospital, but she knew that to provide for her, she had to carve out time for herself.

Scarlett was on the move. As she left the hospital, something didn't feel right, but she could not pinpoint it. She said a quick little prayer to protect Noelle and herself, making sure she wouldn't catch a cold, as that could be detrimental to Noelle's recovery.

Upon entering, Scarlett found a couple of parents who had become acquaintances. Although her life felt like an endless rollercoaster, she knew she was not alone.

Chatter bounced back and forth in the group as they caught up with each other before the meeting.

Nikolas was waiting patiently in the hall, listening to the conversation behind the closed door, waiting for the perfect opportunity to seek out his plan of bumping into Scarlett. Roughly twenty minutes later, everyone was starting to leave. Nicolas ran down the hall to the stairwell. Everyone passed by Nikolas on their way out, but still no sign of Scarlett.

Nikolas scratched his head. Did she pass him without him noticing? Scarlett held her head down and made her way down the stairs. Nikolas grinned, *"It's go time!"* he said with a smile. Nikolas' plan went into action. He looked down and started heading up the stairs to meet her on the landing. With perfect timing, he bumped into Scarlett, knocking her off balance. He wraps his arm around her waist and spins her around to pin her against the wall.

"My apologies," Scarlett said in embarrassment as she looked up, staring deep into Nikolas' eyes for forgiveness. *"Never apologize, having your beauty in my embrace is*

apology enough," Nikolas said in a deep, sultry tone. Scarlett feels a sense of familiarity with Nikolas' embrace and does not move as she feels at home within his arms. *"Your voice sounds familiar."* She mentions. Thrown off by this comment, Nikolas clears his throat, *"It does? Did you put me on your Santa wish list?"* Hoping to trigger her memory. With that comment, realization washes over Scarlett's face after a couple of minutes. *"You played Santa at the hospital!"* Scarlett exclaimed. Nikolas dipped his head down and chuckled. *"Nice surprise running into you here,"* he casually mentions. His urges were getting the best of him, and staring at her luscious lips, he wanted to take Scarlett right there in the stairwell.

His gift under the belt started to grow harder as he was perfectly lined up in Scarlett's gift box. He could easily pick her up and slide right in. The thought of hearing her moans echoing in the stairwell got him close to busting in his pants. There was no denying that Scarlett could feel it. It was apparent he was teasing her with his giant bulge.

Scarlett could feel his giant bulge as it pressed against her. It has been a long time since someone showed her any attention to her lonely, aching gift. Scarlett sneakily spread her legs to feel Nikolas fall further into her canal. The temptation of getting under Scarlett made Nikolas release a low growl into Scarlett's ear. Scarlett lightly touches Nikolas's chin, bringing her lips closer to his, waiting for him to take the bait after hovering for a couple of seconds. Nikolas takes the bait and kisses Scarlett passionately, running his hands down her sides, his hands gripping around Scarlett's perfectly round ass and lifting her. His cock is grinding into her pussy as she is pressed against the wall.

He lets out a moan. *"God, you are sexy, Scarlett. Please say I can have you?"* Nikolas begged. Without skipping a beat, Scarlett answered, *"Take me!"* Nikolas unzipped his pants and moved Scarlett's thong out of the way, sliding himself inside her. Scarlett let out a loud moan, which drove Nikolas insane, making him pound Scarlett harder with each thrust. Her pussy engulfed Nikolas' massive, aching cock. He fought the urge to explode inside her as he wanted to take her longer.

He pulled her head back to expose her beautiful neck, attacking it with his lips, scratching it with his teeth, sending chills down her spine. *"I'm going to explode,"* she said. Nikolas gripped her hips harder and unleashed rapid thrusts deep into Scarlett's pussy. Her moans loudly echoed in the stairwell. Nikolas could not control his excitement anymore. Scarlett milked Nikolas' cock into exploding deep inside her pussy. His juices mixed perfectly with her sweet juices.

With perfect timing, they fixed themselves just as the next group of people began to enter the building. Scarlett shyly smiled at Nikolas while both caught their breath. Nikolas handed Scarlett his phone. *"I need your number."* Scarlett smiled and entered her phone number into his phone. *"You know, I have not done anything like that in a while,"* Scarlett mentions. Nikolas smiles, "Good, that means *I will be a lasting memory.*" He texted the number she provided. Nikolas grabs the back of her neck and pulls her into a deep, passionate kiss as their tongues dance with one another. Scarlett becomes lost in thought, pondering all the possibilities with this man.

When Nikolas pulls away, he whispers in her ear, "*I will be in contact.*" Before walking away.

Scarlett took a deep breath when Nikolas was out of sight. She leaned against the wall and tried to comprehend what had happened, as sexy and thrilling as that encounter was. She could not understand precisely how it happened. Honestly, she couldn't care less, nor did she want to find out. It has been a while since she has been touched, let alone desired by the opposite sex. Given all the stress she had been under, it was necessary. Scarlett felt like she was in a dream.

Chapter Nine
Reminiscing

Later that night, back at the hospital, Scarlett helped Noelle fall asleep. As she sat by the window, the soft glow of the parking lot lights peeked through the blinds. Scarlett wrapped herself up in her blanket. Memories flooded her mind. The aggressive touch of his fingers gripping onto her skin, the way his eyes met with hers with an intensity that spoke volumes without words. Each moan expressed by each other, the moment of vulnerability, all woven together into a tapestry of intimacy that enveloped her head, mind, and soul.

Closing her eyes, Scarlett could almost feel his breath against her neck, sending shivers down her spine. The way he held her close, as if she were the most desired thing in the world. In that moment, everything was at a standstill, as the only thing that mattered was the connection they shared.

She smiled softly, cherishing every detail of their passionate encounter. Though they may be apart for now, the memories they created together will forever remain etched in her soul. The urge to feel that explosion again was tempting Scarlett. But even self-pleasure could not match what she experienced earlier that day.

Nikolas was in his parking spot, looking up to the room that was home to Scarlett and Noelle. He found himself lost in a sea of memories, each one a snapshot of his and Scarlett's afternoon. The soft touch of her hand against his skin, the way her moans filled the air like music, it all came rushing back to him with a bittersweet intensity.

He closed his eyes; he could almost feel her presence beside him. Her warmth welcomed him home in an enveloping embrace. The way she looked at him with those beautiful, longing eyes, desperate to feel desired. Her moans, whispered words, every stolen kiss, all woven together perfectly.

Nikolas sighed, a mixture of longing and gratitude swirling within him. He needed more of Scarlett. As he sat there, reminiscing on their afternoon, he was dedicated to figuring out a game plan to make Scarlett his forever angel.

With a determined furrow in his brow, Nikolas sat up in the car, with a pen in his hand and a notebook in the other, mapping out his game plan to win her heart. Each stroke of the pen on the paper was a calculated move, a strategic step in the intricate dance of winning Scarlett.

He thought of ways to charm her, to make her laugh, to show her the depths of his affection. From romantic gestures to thoughtful surprises, he plotted each move with precision, knowing that every action could bring him closer to his goal.

As he brainstormed, his mind buzzed with ideas, each one more creative than the last. He envisioned their future together, a tapestry of shared adventures and unforgettable moments.

Nikolas had his plan firmly in place. He smiled to himself, confident in his ability to make her heart skip a beat and make her wet between the legs. This was going to be a thrilling adventure waiting to unfold. Temptation arose as Nikolas sat there with his eyes fixated on the window through which Scarlett was sleeping. His heart raced with anticipation as he longed to watch her peaceful slumber;

his obsession was driving him closer to the edge of insanity. He couldn't tear his gaze away. The desire to witness Scarlett's every subtle movement of her sleeping figure consumed Nikolas entirely.

He needed to have her, more of her!

Chapter Ten
Shopping

Nikolas' alarm went off, startling him to wake up. In a panic, he hit the car horn. He fell asleep in the parking lot last night. After he gathered his bearings, he quickly drove back home to get ready for the day. He had to take care of another Angel.

Back at the hospital, a soft morning light filtered from behind the curtains. Scarlett stirred from her restless night of sleep. When she woke, her eyes were heavy with exhaustion. She tossed and turned all night thinking about Nikolas. With a heavy heart, she glanced over at Noelle, lying in the hospital bed, doing her best to fight cancer.

Weariness etched deep lines on Scarlett's face as she mustered the strength to rise; her maternal instinct started to push through. She had to be the pillar of strength for her child despite the overwhelming fatigue that weighed her down. Scarlett took a deep breath, steeling herself for another day of battling alongside Noelle. Today was going to be long, as it was chemo day.

Back at Nikolas' house under the cascade of water, Nikolas let the steam envelop him. His thoughts were consumed by the woman he couldn't shake from his mind. As rivulets of water trickled down his body, he closed his eyes, envisioning Scarlett's delicate features and the curve of her smile. The memory of her lingered in his thoughts like an unrelenting echo; each droplet of water was a reminder of his insatiable obsession. Lost in his thoughts, his cock became hard.

His fingers gripping his base, stroking up and down nice and slow, savoring every stroke, his hand squeezing here and there to mimic the pulse of Scarlett's tight, wet pussy. Nikolas lost balance and held onto the wall of the shower as he stroked harder and faster, reminiscing about when he was pounding Scarlett in the stairwell. He recalled her moans as he neared completion. A smile danced across his lips as a huge load exploded out of the head of his cock and splattered onto the wall.

The water started to turn cold as he finished cleaning up himself and his mess. Nikolas thought to himself, *"No one could ever compare to Scarlett."*

Nikolas saw the time and started to rush; he was running behind schedule. With his heart pounding, adrenaline coursing through his veins, Nikolas dashed through the crowded city streets. His eyes fixed on his watch as the minutes ticked away mercilessly. Sidestepping pedestrians and dodging traffic, he weaved through the bustling throng, his determination unyielding. Each step propelled him closer to his next angel.

Upon arriving at the destination where his angel was supposed to be. Nikolas was breathless and eager to help his angel. He scanned the area, only to freeze in disbelief at the sight before him. There, standing arm in arm with another man, was the angel he had been seeking out. Shock coursed through him. Standing still like a statue, he watched them laugh and share intimate glances.

In that moment, the world froze in time. He never had misinformation; all the angels he seeks out are lonely and needy. He thought to himself, "Could Scarlett be throwing me off my game?" Lost and confused in the chaotic cityscape, Nikolas could not rejoice in helping this angel out. As the man she was with was a well-known shark in the corporate world.

Although Nikolas was confused about the situation, and knew this angel would be taken care of. Deep down in his heart, he still felt obligated to make sure the child was taken care of. Off he went to fulfil the Christmas wish list for the child who wanted nothing but little race cars, dinosaurs, and magnetic tiles.

Chapter Eleven
Gameplan

After dropping off the presents for the Angel, Nikolas stood there next to his car, tapping the hood, pondering. His mind was a whirlwind of strategy, trying to craft the perfect scenario to "accidentally" run into Scarlett. He considered her daily routine, where she could be located today, and how he could naturally appear in those spaces without seeming too eager or worse, her catching on that he was stalking her.

He had a broad idea of how Noelle was doing, but was not too positive about what her treatment consisted of. Nikolas was tempted to "accidentally" bump into her at the hospital, as it was the safest bet she would be there. But how could his master plan work? After a couple of minutes, a light bulb went off in Nikolas's head.

It was the perfect plan. Nikolas quickly set off for the hospital. Nikolas dashed to the hospital gift shop; he quickly scanned the shelves before settling on the small selection of flowers. Time was of the essence, and he moved with a purpose, quickly picking out a bouquet that caught his eye. A vibrant mix of colors, lively and hopeful. When he laid his eyes upon the bouquet, he could envision the smile it might bring to Scarlett.

At the counter, he paid with haste that betrayed his calm exterior. Nikolas paused just outside the swinging doors that led to the Oncology Floor. He adjusted a couple of stems, ensuring the bouquet looked its best. With the flowers now in hand, he was ready to step back into the corridor. The urgency in his stride softened as he made his way through the halls, searching for Scarlett.

Scarlett came from around the corner, almost colliding with Nikolas. *"Oh no, my apologies! I was not paying attention,"* Scarlett said. She held on to Nikolas' arms to make sure he did not drop anything. *"If it was anyone's fault, it was mine, beautiful,"* Nikolas said with a charming smile as his free hand lay upon Scarlett's hand. Scarlett blushed, *"Those flowers are stunning! You are going to make your special someone's day with those."* Nikolas smiled and handed the flowers to Scarlett. *"Well, I hope they make you feel special. They are for you."*

Stunned by his comment, Scarlett took a step back. *"Me? No. I couldn't."* She stared at Nikolas, trying to figure out where she recognized him from. *"My grandfather, who raised me, would be highly disappointed if I did not give a beautiful woman such as yourself a beautiful bouquet to remind her of how beautiful she is. So, you are doing me the honors of accepting these flowers, and I'm getting to tell my grandfather he raised me right."* Nikolas said in a persuasive tone.

Scarlett smiled and accepted the flowers. *"Tell your grandfather he raised you right. I am glad to bump into you since our stairwell encounter. I am surprised to see you here."* Scarlett mentioned. Nikolas tried to keep the smug look under control and had to think quickly. *"Surprised? Why is that?"* he said. Scarlett became nervous, twiddling her thumbs. *"I didn't know you had a family member fighting as well."* Nikolas took a step towards her, looking down at her face. *"If you feel alone, stop, you will never be alone."* He said in a whisper.

Just then, a nurse came around the corner, interrupting them. *"Scarlett, your daughter is asking for you."* The nurse said with urgency. Scarlett squeezed Nikolas's hand before dashing off to see what the matter was with Noelle. Standing in the hallway, Nikolas looked down at his hand that was still pulsating from her gentle squeeze.

While medical staff shuffled past him, a satisfying grin played across Nikola's lips as he stared at his hand.

Deep in his mind, a sense of triumph blossomed as he reveled in the success of his meticulously crafted plan to make Scarlett fall for him. Each subtle gesture, every carefully chosen word, had worked like a charm, and now, seeing her warm response, he felt a surge of happiness knowing that his strategy was unfolding exactly as he had envisioned.

Chapter Twelve
Chemo

In the sterile hospital room, little Noelle sat on her bed, her tiny frame engulfed by the oversized hospital gown. Her once vibrant curls have now thinned. A testament to the toll chemotherapy had taken on her fragile body. With wide eyes, she watched as the nurse approached with a gentle smile, holding a syringe filled with medication.

Thankfully, Mom came around her and was there to support her during this time. Noelle's small hand trembled as the needle pierced her skin, tears welling up in her eyes. Despite the discomfort, her brave spirit shone through as she whispered to her mother, *"It's okay, Mommy. I'm strong."* As the medication flowed into her veins, Noelle closed her eyes, clinging to hope amidst the harsh reality of her battle against cancer.

Noelle sat back in her hospital bed, staring at colorful drawings and cards. She has been fighting cancer with remarkable resilience. With bright eyes and a hopeful smile, she turned to her nurse, who had become a dear friend during her stay. *"You know, Ms. Cali,"* she began, her voice tinged with excitement, *"I just can't wait to be done with all these treatments. I want to be home for Christmas, celebrating with my family, not stuck in this hospital bed."* Ms. Cali nodded empathetically, her heart swelling with admiration for the brave little girl before her. *"I know, Noelle,"* she replied gently, reaching out to squeeze her hand. *"You've been so powerful throughout all of this. I'm sure Christmas will be extraordinary this year."*

Noelle's eyes sparkled with determination as she nodded in agreement. *"Oh, it will be, Miss Cali! We'll have the biggest Christmas tree, and I'll make sure to leave extra cookies for Santa. And maybe, just maybe, I'll even get to go sledding if it snows!"*

As Noelle shared her dreams of the perfect Christmas at home, the room filled with warmth and hope. Despite the challenges she faced, her spirit remained unbroken, her resolve unwavering. With each passing day, she moved one step closer to family, celebrating the most magical time of the year in the place where she truly belonged.

Scarlett sat by her daughter's bedside, her eyes filled with a mix of love and concern. Her daughter, Noelle, chatted animatedly with the nurse, her voice infused with a determination that belied her tender age.

As Noelle expressed her longing to be home for Christmas, Scarlett watched. Her heart was heavy with the weight of their circumstances. She listened intently as her daughter spoke, marveling at the strength and resilience that radiated from her small frame.

Nurse Cali nodded in understanding, her expression calm and reassuring, compassion evident in the gentle touch of her hand on Noelle's shoulder. Scarlett felt a surge of gratitude for the care and support Nurse Cali had provided throughout their journey.

Though her own heart ached with the desire to grant her daughter's wish, Scarlett knew that Noelle's battle against cancer was far from over. Yet, in that moment, as she witnessed the unwavering determination in Noelle's eyes, she couldn't help but feel a glimmer of hope.

With a tender smile, Scarlett reached out to brush a stray strand of hair from Noelle's forehead, the love for her daughter overflowing. Together, they would weather this storm, clinging to the promise of brighter days ahead and the hope of celebrating Christmas at home, surrounded by the warmth and love of their family.

When Nurse Cali left the hospital room, Scarlett sat beside her daughter's bed, her expression was a mix of tenderness and reassurance. Noelle lay propped up against pillows, her face drawn with fatigue yet illuminated by a flicker of hope.

"It's okay, my love," Scarlett murmured, her voice soft and soothing. *"I know it's not what we planned, but we'll make the best of it. Even if we spend Christmas in the hospital, it can still be special."*

Noelle gazed up at her mother, her eyes reflecting a myriad of emotions - uncertainty, disappointment, but also a glimmer of acceptance. *"But I wanted to be home for Christmas,"* she whispered; her voice fragile with longing.

Scarlett reached out, gently grasping Noelle's hand in her own. "*I know, darling,*" she said, her voice trembling slightly with emotion. "*But what matters most is that we're together. We'll decorate your room, and we'll have a small tree, and we'll make it as festive as we can.*"

Noelle's lips curved into a faint smile, her heart touched by her mother's unwavering love and support. "*Okay,*" she whispered, a sense of peace settling over her.

As they sat together in the quiet of the hospital room, Scarlett and Noelle found solace in each other's presence. Despite the challenges they faced, they knew that their bond would carry them through, infusing even the darkest of days with light and hope. And as they looked ahead to Christmas in the hospital, they embraced the promise of love, resilience, and the enduring spirit of the holiday season.

Chapter Thirteen

Fallen Angel

As the evening sun cast a warm glow through the window of his home, Nikolas stood before the mirror, adjusting his tie with care. Tonight was the night he had been looking forward to for weeks. A shopping spree with another Angel. This woman, whom he had grown to admire, enjoyed the silly tactics her son used to bring a smile to her face. His heart fluttered with excitement as he imagined the evening ahead: shopping, laughter, and of course, the end of the treatment, a happy ending.

Just as he reached for his coat, the familiar sound of the television caught his attention. Turning towards the screen, he watched in disbelief as the news anchor's somber voice filled the room, reporting on a recent incident downtown. His heart sank as he listened to the details unfold – a young woman, the victim of a brutal attack, her name echoing in his mind like a haunting refrain.

Frozen in shock, Nikolas felt a surge of fear and dread wash over him. Could it be...? With trembling hands, he reached for his phone, his fingers fumbling as he dialed her number, desperate for reassurance, for confirmation that she was safe.

As the phone rang, each passing second felt like an eternity, until finally, a familiar voice answered on the other end. Heartbreak flooded through Nikolas as he listened to her son's words, his voice trembling with emotion as he cried out, "My mommy is dead!" The cries echoed through Nikolas's ears.

The phone lay cradled in the trembling hand of Nikolas, his heart heavy with dread as he listened to the boy's voice on the other end of the line. His mind reeled in disbelief, struggling to comprehend the words that shattered his world – the devastating news of the loss of an Angel, a mother, leaving behind a young child all alone in this evil world.

Little Jack sat huddled on the couch, gripping his mom's phone, his face pale and eyes wide with pain as he clutched a stuffed toy tightly to his chest. His world had been upended in an instant, the comforting embrace of his mother torn away, leaving him adrift in a sea of grief and confusion.

With a heavy sigh, Nikolas tried to get Jack's attention. "Jack, buddy, I need you to listen to me. Is *anyone there with you?*" Jack sniffled as he tried to catch his breath from crying hysterically, "No! A woman in a suit is taking me away from Mommy!" he cried out. Nikolas' heart ached knowing that he would be in the system soon. His mom left everything behind, seeking a different life for herself and Jack. She left an abusive home life to break the generational curse, and it backfired on her. Ripping her away from her pride and joy.

Nikolas fought back tears and cleared his throat. "Can you put the lady in the suit on the phone, please, Jack?" Jack's cries echo as he hands the phone off. *"Hi ma'am, my name is Nikolas, and I am a good friend of Jack and his mother. Will he be ok?"* Nikolas asked. Calmly, the woman answers, "Hi Nikolas, I am sorry we are talking under these circumstances. Until we can find out who did this and if there was a will, Jack will be going into foster placement until we find a family *or a close friend that Jack could go to. Right now, Jack needs to process this and get the help he needs."* Nikolas was too stunned during the conversation; he forgot to ask for the caseworker's name. Pacing the floor of his house. He had never dealt with an Angel being viciously taken away before.

Nikolas sat slumped at the kitchen table, a heavy weight pressing down on his shoulders. His hands trembled as he raised the glass to his lips, the amber liquid burning his throat as he swallowed it down, seeking solace in the numbness it promised.

The words echoed in his ears, *"My mommy is dead!"* haunted him. Nikolas felt that he had failed them, failed to keep them safe from harm, and now they were gone – the mother lost to the merciless grasp of death, the child swallowed up by the impersonal machinery of the foster care system. A bitter taste filled Nikolas' mouth as he slammed the glass down onto the table, the sharp clang echoing in the empty room. The world was a cruel and unforgiving place, and try as he might, he could not shield those who needed it most.

With a heavy sigh, Nikolas leaned back in his chair, his gaze fixed on the ceiling above as he wrestled with the demons that gnawed at his soul. The weight of this fallen Angel bore down on him like a suffocating blanket, crushing him beneath its relentless burden. And so, he drank, drowning his sorrows in the amber depths of the bottle, seeking refuge from the pain that threatened to consume him whole.

For in the numbing embrace of alcohol, he found a fleeting respite from the relentless ache of guilt and regret that gnawed at his heart, a reprieve from the crushing weight of being too late.

Chapter Fourteen
Shadows

As the first tendrils of dawn began to creep through the city streets, Nikolas stirred restlessly in his bed, his head throbbing with the dull ache of a hangover. With a groan, he reluctantly peeled his heavy eyelids open, his vision blurred and unfocused as he tried to make sense of the world around him.

Memories from the previous night flooded back with painful clarity – the numbing embrace of alcohol, the bitter taste of regret, the haunting echo of little Jack's cries. And above all else, the image of her – the woman he was falling deeply in love with, her face etched with worry and sorrow as she stood vigil by her daughter's bedside in the hospital.

Driven by a potent mix of longing and desperation, Nikolas swung his legs over the edge of the bed, his movements slow and unsteady as he rose to his feet. With a shaky hand, he reached for his coat, his mind consumed by a singular purpose – to see her, to be near her, if only for a fleeting moment.

The streets were deserted as Nikolas stumbled into the cold, pre-dawn darkness, the chill air biting at his skin as he made his way towards the hospital. His steps faltered and were unsteady, his mind clouded by the remnants of an alcohol-induced haze, but still he pressed on, driven by an insatiable need to be close to her.

Nikolas neared the hospital, and a sense of anticipation mingled with trepidation came washing over him, his heart pounding in his chest as he approached the entrance. With bated breath, he pushed open the heavy doors, the familiar scent of antiseptic and sterile cleanliness enveloping him like a suffocating shroud.

And there she was, just as he had imagined – the woman he had become obsessed with, her eyes heavy with exhaustion, her features drawn and weary as she sat vigil by her daughter's bedside. For a moment, Nikolas stood frozen in place, his heart aching with longing as he watched her from the shadows, his presence unnoticed in the dimly lit hospital room.

But even as he gazed upon her, a gnawing sense of guilt and shame clawed at his conscience, a stark reminder of the selfishness of his actions. He had no right to intrude upon her grief, no right to impose himself upon her world in such a reckless and thoughtless manner. Nikolas had a constant battle between his urges and guilt.

He wanted to rush into that room and embrace his Angel. From the hallway, he could see that Noelle was not doing well, and at that moment, he knew that his urge would be a burden too heavy to bear for Scarlett. So, Nikolas walked back to the car to sit and watch from afar.

Back in the hospital room, Scarlett sat by Noelle's bedside, her eyes fixed on the peaceful rise and fall of her daughter's chest as she slept. Noelle, her precious daughter, lay curled up beneath the soft hospital blankets, her face serene in repose, her battle with cancer momentarily forgotten in the embrace of sleep. As Scarlett watched over her daughter, a sense of exhaustion weighed heavily on her shoulders, the relentless strain of worry and fear etched into the lines of her face. Yet, despite the weariness that tugged at her bones, she remained steadfast by Noelle's side, her love unwavering and unyielding. But as Scarlett sat in the dimly lit room, a prickling sensation crept up the back of her neck, a nagging feeling that she was not alone. She glanced around the room, her senses on high alert as she searched for the source of her unease. She peeked out the curtains to see a parking lot bustling with people heading home.

As she glanced down, she noticed a shadowy figure lurking in the car seat. Scarlett's heart skipped a beat as she stared at the car. Catching her breath, her trembling hand quickly jotted down the car's license plate and description. Exhaustion overwhelmed Scarlett; she turned to watch over her daughter, bathed in the soft glow of the bedside lamp. She felt a deep-seated fear and paranoia of being watched.

Who could it be? One thing she knew for sure was that it was not Noelle's father; he had made it clear that they would never see or hear from him again.

Nikolas sat in his car, his heart racing with a mixture of anticipation and fear. He peered cautiously through the window, his breath catching in his throat as he caught sight of Scarlett. As he watched Scarlett's actions in the window, he knew she had written down the car information. Nikolas couldn't shake the feeling of guilt that gnawed at his conscience. He knew he shouldn't be here, shouldn't be spying on them like some voyeur, but he couldn't resist the pull of his emotions, the longing to be close to the Angel he was falling deeply for.

Panic surged through him like a tidal wave, his stomach lurching as he realized he might have been caught in the act. He cursed himself for his foolishness, for allowing his emotions to cloud his judgment and betray the trust of the very people he had set out to help.

As he hurried away from the hospital, Nikolas couldn't shake the feeling of guilt that clung to him like a shadow, a constant reminder of the boundaries he had crossed and the consequences of his actions. And yet, despite his remorse, a small part of him couldn't help but feel a glimmer of excitement that Scarlett was possibly going to catch him, and he could stop hiding. Nikolas smacked himself back into reality. "You damn fool, stay with the game plan." He murmured.

Chapter Fifteen

Turn for the Worst

While making paper snowflakes to hang in the hospital room, Scarlett sat by Noelle's bedside, her exhaustion palpable in the heavy lines etched across her face. Noelle is fragile, but she is determined to celebrate Christmas traditions through her never-ending yawns and naps.

As Scarlett watched over her daughter, a sense of helplessness washed over her like a tidal wave, threatening to engulf her in its suffocating embrace. No matter how hard she tried to push back the tide of despair, it seemed to crash over her again and again, leaving her battered and bruised in its wake.

But even in the depths of her despair, Scarlett couldn't shake the nagging tug of guilt that gnawed at her conscience. She had promised herself that she would attend the support group meeting tonight, seeking solace and understanding from others who shared her burden.

Yet here she was, unable to tear herself away from Noelle's side, her heart torn between the desperate need for support and the fierce determination to be there for her daughter no matter what.

With a heavy sigh, Scarlett glanced at the clock on the wall, the hands ticking relentlessly forward, each passing moment a painful reminder of the choice she had to make. She longed to be with the other parents, to share her fears and frustrations, to find comfort in their shared experiences. And yet, she couldn't bear the thought of leaving Noelle alone, even for just a few hours.

As the internal struggle waged war within her, Scarlett felt a familiar ache welling up inside her. The relentless pull of mom guilt, that insidious voice whispering in her ear that she was failing her daughter, that she wasn't doing enough, that she should be able to handle it all on her own.

But as she looked at Noelle, so small and fragile in her hospital bed, Scarlett knew that she couldn't let her guilt dictate her actions. Noelle needed her now more than ever. Noelle needed her love and her strength to help her through this darkest of times.

With a determined resolve, Scarlett pushed aside her doubts and fears, steeling herself for the long night ahead. She might not be able to attend the support group meeting tonight, but she would find a way to pull through, to be there for Noelle in body and in spirit, to weather this storm together as a family, come what may.

Noelle lay still upon her bed, her small frame seeming even more fragile in the harsh glare of the overhead lights. The steady beep of the monitors provided a monotonous backdrop to the otherwise silent room, punctuated only by the occasional shuffle of nurses outside in the corridor.

But beneath the veneer of calm, a storm brewed within Noelle's body. The cancer treatment, meant to be a beacon of hope in her battle against the insidious disease, had instead become a relentless adversary, wreaking havoc on her already weakened immune system.

As the minutes stretched into hours, a feeling of unease settled over Noelle, a creeping sense of discomfort that seemed to coil itself around her like a suffocating embrace. She shifted restlessly in her bed, her brow furrowing in a silent plea for relief from the relentless onslaught of nausea and pain.

And then came a wave of sickness so intense it felt as though her very insides were being torn asunder. Noelle clutched at her stomach; her fingers were white-knuckled with the effort to hold back the tide of agony that threatened to overwhelm her.

Her breath came into ragged gasps as she fought to maintain control, to keep the churning storm within her at bay. But try as she might, the sickness continued to claw at her, its relentless grip tightening with each passing moment.

Outside the room, the nurses hurried to Noelle's side, their voices a soothing balm amidst the chaos of her distress. They moved with practiced efficiency, administering medications and adjusting IV lines in a desperate bid to quell the storm raging within her.

And slowly, gradually, the storm began to subside, its fury tempered by the steady hand of medical intervention. Noelle's breathing eased, her body relaxing as the worst of the sickness passed, leaving her drained and exhausted in its wake.

As she lay there, spent and weary, Noelle couldn't help but wonder how much more of this she could endure. But amidst the darkness of her despair, a flicker of hope remained. The hope that one day, she would emerge from this storm stronger than before, ready to face whatever challenges lay ahead in her journey towards healing and recovery.

Chapter Sixteen
Sparkies

A couple of days passed, and Noelle's fragile body began to regain a little strength. Grandma had one goal today, and that was to put a smile on her precious little Noelle's face. A knock on the door, and as it opens, Grandma chimes in, *"Oh, little Noelle, are you ready for a surprise?"* she says with a joyful tone. Noelle whipped her head around in excitement as she heard Grandma's voice, *"Grandma!"* Her eyes became large as she looked at the bag of goodies that Grandma was carrying into the room. *"Is that what I think it is?"* questioned Noelle. *"Depends on Noelle, what do you think it is?"* Grandma answered. *"Cookies?"* Noelle screeched with excitement, reaching for the bags of goodies. Scarlett sat back in her chair, admiring her daughter's happiness while she answered emails.

The room filled with the soft hum of medical equipment and Christmas music playing, a small table was adorned with trays of plain sugar cookies and an array of colorful icing tubes. The sunlight filtered gently through the window, casting a warm glow on the scene within.

Noelle was seated at the table, her face adorned with a bright smile that seemed to light up the room. Beside her stood Grandma, her weathered hands guiding Noelle's hesitant movements as she piped the vibrant icing. Grandma's eyes sparkled with love and tenderness as she watched her granddaughter's concentration, her heart swelling with pride at the simple joy of this moment.

Across from them, Scarlett sat there, her laptop open in front of her as she balanced the demands of work with the desire to be present for her daughter. Despite the distractions of her inbox, her gaze frequently flickered up to take in the scene before her, a soft smile playing on her lips at the sight of Noelle's happiness.

As the trio worked together, laughter filled the room, mingling with the sweet scent of sugar and icing. Noelle's hands were soon stained with a kaleidoscope of colors as she decorated each cookie with care, her imagination running wild with the possibilities.

In that moment, surrounded by love and laughter, the worries of the outside world seemed to fade away, replaced by the simple joy of being together. And, as they shared in the delight of decorating cookies, the bonds of family grew even stronger, weaving a tapestry of memories that would be cherished for years to come.

Suddenly, a knock on the door interrupted them; it was Nurse Cali. *"Time for vitals, bestie."* She mentions as she puts on her stethoscope. Noelle let out a sigh. *"Well, it felt like I was out of the hospital for a moment."* Scarlett's joy of seeing Noelle happy turned into a mission. As an idea came to her mind, *"Noelle, baby, how about we get a special lunch today? Grandma can watch you while I run to get it?"* Before Scarlett could finish her sentence, Noelle interrupted her, *"Sparkies!"* Scarlett chuckled as she saw Noelle get excited again. Shaking her head in agreement, *"Yes, Sparkies."* Noelle was jumping out of excitement, messing up Nurse Cali's vital intake.

A couple of hours passed by, and a yawn escaped from Noelle. As she fights to stay awake, Grandma gets into bed with her to cuddle her for an early afternoon catnap.

Scarlett shut her laptop and gathered her purse, quietly walking over to Noelle to kiss her forehead as she headed out to get Noelle's favorite lunch.

In the parking lot, Nikolas sat behind the wheel of his car, idling in the parking lot of the hospital, lost in his own thoughts. His eyes wandered absently over the passing cars and bustling pedestrians, but his mind was elsewhere, preoccupied with the events of the day. Suddenly, his attention was drawn to a figure emerging from the hospital entrance.

It was Scarlett. She moved with purpose, her long strides carrying her swiftly across the parking lot. As Scarlett reached her car, Nikolas felt a surge of adrenaline course through him. Without conscious thought, he found himself reaching for the gear shift, his instincts urging him to follow her. With a glance around to ensure he wouldn't attract attention, he shifted into gear and pulled out of the parking spot, falling into step behind Scarlett's car.

 As they navigated the busy streets, Nikolas kept a safe distance, careful not to draw too close. He watched intently as Scarlett drove her expression unreadable behind the tinted windows of her car. His curiosity burned within him, driving him to follow her wherever she might lead. Minutes turned into miles as they wound through the city, Nikolas trailing behind like a silent shadow. Despite the uncertainty of his actions, he couldn't shake the feeling of excitement that coursed through him. He was drawn to Scarlett, drawn to the mystery that surrounded her.

Eventually, Scarlett's car came to a stop outside a quaint diner nestled on a quiet street corner. Nikolas parked a discreet distance away, watching as she disappeared inside. For a moment, he hesitated, unsure of what to do next. But the pull of curiosity was too strong to resist. With a determined resolve, Nikolas stepped out of his car and followed Scarlett into the diner, ready to uncover the secrets that lay hidden beneath her enigmatic exterior.

Nikolas pushed open the door to the diner, the familiar chime of the bell announcing his arrival. The scent of freshly brewed coffee and sizzling bacon enveloped him as he stepped inside, the warmth of the cozy establishment offering a welcome respite from the chill of the outside world. His eyes swept over the room, taking in the rows of booths and the scattered tables occupied by diners engaged in quiet conversation. And then, at the counter, he saw her. Scarlett stood there, her back turned to him as she leaned against the counter, engrossed in perusing the menu displayed above. Her long, dark hair cascaded in loose waves down her back, framing her delicate features with an air of effortless elegance.

Nikolas felt a jolt of recognition shoot through him as he watched her, his heart quickening in his chest. With a sense of determination, Nikolas made his way across the diner, his footsteps echoing softly against the tiled floor. He approached the counter where Scarlett stood, his gaze fixed on her as he drew nearer.

As Scarlett turned from placing her order, her eyes met his, and for a moment, time seemed to stand still. There was a flicker of recognition in her gaze, a spark of curiosity mirrored in her eyes. *"Can I help you?"* the waitress behind the counter asked, breaking the spell that had fallen over them.

Nikolas cleared his throat, his voice steady as he replied, "*I'll have what she's having,*" nodding towards Scarlett with a small smile. Scarlett chuckled with amusement. *"I'm not sure you would like what a 5-year-old is having."* He settled onto the stool beside her. Nikolas couldn't help but feel that fate had brought them together once again, weaving their paths together in a way that felt inevitable and right. He chuckled and quickly had to change the subject. "Didn't see you as a Sparkies fan," said Nikolas. Scarlett sat beside him. "My daughter loves it here; she has been in a massive slump, *having to spend Christmas in the hospital. We decorated cookies earlier, thanks to my mom, and I figured, why not get lunch at her favorite spot?*" Scarlett spoke with a bit of exhaustion in her tone. "*You are an incredible mother, plus you can't beat their onion rings,*" Nikolas said in a cheerful tone.

The two of them chatted while their orders were prepped. Nikolas shifted in his seat next to Scarlett, the soft glow of the overhead lights casting a warm ambiance around them. Their orders are being placed in the pickup window. Nikolas knew his window of time was closing in. With each passing moment, Nikolas found himself drawn deeper into Scarlett's presence, captivated by the easy way she laughed and the sparkle in her eyes. He knew that he couldn't let this opportunity slip away, that he had to take a chance and ask her out. Summoning his courage, Nikolas cleared his throat, drawing Scarlett's attention away from their conversation. *"Scarlett,"* he began, his voice steady despite the nervous flutter in his chest, *"I've really enjoyed spending this brief time with you today."* A soft smile tugged at Scarlett's lips as she met his gaze, her eyes warm and inviting. *"I've enjoyed it too, Nikolas,"* she replied, her voice soft and sincere. Emboldened by her response, Nikolas pressed on, his words tumbling out in a rush. *"I was wondering if, maybe, you'd like to go out with me sometime. You know, for dinner or... or something."*

There was a moment of silence as Scarlett considered his invitation, her expression thoughtful. Then, to Nikolas's relief, a smile spread across her face, lighting up her features with warmth. *"I would love to,"* she said, her voice filled with genuine enthusiasm. "*I think that would be wonderful.*" A sense of elation washed over Nikolas as he realized that she had accepted his invitation. He couldn't help but smile, his heart soaring with joy at the prospect of spending more time with her. As they made plans to meet again, Nikolas couldn't shake the feeling that this was just the beginning of something truly special. And as they parted ways, he knew that he was already looking forward to their subsequent encounter, eager to see where this new connection might lead.

Back at the hospital, Scarlett was beaming with excitement about their date, but her smile widened even more at the thought of Noelle's reaction to her lunch. Quietly entering the room, she finds Grandma awake, cuddling Noelle as she sleeps. Scarlett nervously set down the items and whispered, "*Mom, do you think you can watch Noelle one afternoon?*" Grandma was shocked by her question, "Of course, *dear, is everything alright?*"

A smile lit up Scarlett's face as she placed the food on the tray. "*I was asked out on a date,*" Scarlett said softly. Grandma's eyes widened as she was thrilled that her daughter was going on a date. *"Of course."* Grandma excitedly says.

Noelle stirred from her catnap, blinking groggily as she slowly regained awareness of her surroundings. The soft light filtering through the curtains indicated that some time had passed since she'd dozed off, but the room still felt warm and cozy. As she stretched and yawned, Noelle's gaze fell upon the bedside table, where a delightful sight awaited her.

There, sitting neatly on a plate, was her favorite indulgence: a Sparkies chicken quesadilla. The aroma of melted cheese and seasoned chicken wafted through the air, tempting her senses and stirring her appetite. Next to the quesadilla sat a small, delectable-looking cupcake, its frosting swirled into a delicate pattern that spoke of sweet indulgence.

Noelle's mouth watered at the sight of it, her stomach rumbling in anticipation. With a delighted grin, Noelle reached for the plate and cupcake, relishing the warmth of the quesadilla in her hand and the softness of the cupcake wrapper beneath her fingertips. She took a moment to savor the moment, reveling in the simple pleasure of waking up to find her favorite treats waiting for her. She took her first bite of the quesadilla, and the flavors exploded on her tongue, filling her with a sense of contentment and satisfaction. And as she followed it up with a bite of the cupcake, the sweetness of the frosting melted away any lingering traces of drowsiness, leaving her feeling fully awake and energized. With each delicious bite, Noelle couldn't help but feel grateful for the thoughtful gesture. It was the perfect pick-me-up after her nap, a reminder that sometimes, life's simplest pleasures were the most satisfying of all.

Scarlett sat back, watching Noelle devour her favorite lunch. Her heart was filled with happiness as she watched her eat, and she was excited knowing she had a date with Nikolas.

Chapter Seventeen
Date

As the sun dipped beneath the horizon, casting a warm glow over the city, Scarlett stood before the bathroom mirror, nerves fluttering like trapped butterflies in her stomach. She smoothed down the fabric of her favorite dress, the one that hugged her curves just right, and applied a touch of lipstick, trying to quell the flutter of excitement mixed with anxiety. Tonight, she was going on a date with Nikolas.

Meanwhile, in the softly lit hospital room, Grandma sat by Noelle's bedside, her weathered hands clasped around the small, fragile hand of her beloved grandchild. Tubes and wires connected the child to various machines, humming quietly. Grandma offered a comforting smile, whispering words of love and reassurance to her little Noelle, who fought so bravely. Scarlett's heart skipped a beat as she heard her phone ring. Nikolas was waiting in the lobby. With one last glance in the mirror, she took a deep breath, mustering

the courage to step out and embrace the night ahead.
Before leaving, Scarlett gave Noelle a kiss and a hug and
thanked her mom for watching her.

As Scarlett and Nikolas greeted each other with smiles
and nervous laughter, Scarlett felt a sense of warmth
wash over her, a feeling that she had not felt in a while.

Together, they embarked on their evening adventure,
the city alive with the promise of endless possibilities.
They shared stories, laughter, and dreams, their
connection deepening with each passing moment.
Scarlett found herself drawn to Nikolas' easy charm and
genuine kindness, while he was captivated by her wit and
grace.

As the night wore on, they found themselves lost in each
other's company, the rest of the world fading into the
background. It was as if they were the only two people in
existence, their hearts beating in perfect harmony. In
that moment, beneath the starlit sky, both Scarlett and
Nikolas dared to believe that they had found something
truly special.

While sparks flew like Fourth of July fireworks, they made their way back to Nikolas' place. Approaching the gated grand entrance was a sweeping driveway lined with meticulously manicured shrubs, leading them towards the imposing facade of the mansion. Towering palm trees swayed gently in the breeze, casting dappled shadows across the pristine white walls, while ornate fountains whispered tales of luxury and extravagance. Scarlett was amazed by the luxurious home standing before her. She was hesitant to enter, feeling like she didn't belong. Nikolas laced his fingers with hers and whispered, *"Come with me."* She shook her head and followed his lead.

Inside the house, Nikolas went to the liquor cabinet and pulled out the finest champagne and lit candles in the living room. In their hands, glasses of champagne sparkled like liquid gold, the effervescent bubbles rising to the surface with each gentle sip. The taste was sweet on their lips, a perfect accompaniment to the warmth and intimacy of the moment.

In the soft glow of the candlelight, Nikolas and Scarlett swayed together in perfect harmony, the strains of a timeless melody filling the air. Their movements were graceful, each step a testament to the deep connection they shared, as they moved as one across the living room floor. The room was bathed in a warm, golden hue, the flickering flames casting dancing shadows against the walls. The gentle notes of a piano floated through the air, intertwining with the soft laughter and whispered words exchanged between the couple. As they danced, Nikolas held Scarlett close, his arms wrapped around her waist in a tender embrace. Her head rested against his chest, her heart beating in time with his own, as they moved together in a silent symphony of love and longing.

With each twirl and dip, their love seemed to deepen, weaving itself into the very fabric of their souls. In that fleeting moment, nothing else mattered but the two of them, lost in the magic of the music and the intensity of their emotions. As the song reached its crescendo, Nikolas pulled Scarlett closer, his lips brushing against hers in a tender kiss.

Time seemed to stand still as they lingered in each other's embrace, savoring the sweetness of the moment and the depth of their connection. In the quiet of the night, as the music faded into silence and the last drops of champagne were savored, Nikolas and Scarlett remained locked in each other's arms, their love shining brightly amidst the flickering candlelight. Nikolas leaned into the nook of Scarlett's neck and softly kissed her neck, his stubble tickling her lightly as chills appeared down her arms, turning Scarlett on as she pulled Nikolas closer to her.

A soft moan escaped her parted lips. Nikolas' hands roamed Scarlett's body, his hands gripping her curves, pulling her dress up as he nips at her neck with teasing bites. Scarlett unbuttons Nikolas's dress shirt, fighting every urge to devour her. He slips Scarlett's dress off. Kissing her passionately, Nikolas pulls away to admire her body exposed in the sexiest black lace lingerie. His eyes roll to the back of his head as he cannot control his urges. He picks Scarlett up as she wraps her legs around him, kissing her passionately and taking her to his bedroom to throw her down on the bed.

Admiring the Angel on his bed, his throbbing cock wanting to break through his pants. Nikolas hooks his arms under her slender legs and plunges his mouth onto her beautiful pussy, savoring her delicious taste as he licks her slowly, devouring her lips. Massaging her clit with his tongue, sucking hard, Scarlett's hips buck up, making her moan louder. Nikolas' throbbing cock couldn't take it anymore. He slipped off his pants. He was wearing red satin boxers, pulling his cock out, he climbed up Scarlett's body, staring deep into her soul as he shoves his cock deep into Scarlett's tight, wet pussy. Thrusting slowly into her. Her moans surrounded Nikolas, echoing all around him. Scarlett's eyes rolled to the back of her head as she got closer to climaxing. Nikolas then turns her around onto all fours, kissing up her back, growling into her ear.

"Grab the fucking headboard." He demands. Scarlett grabs the headboard while Nikolas spreads her voluptuous ass, thrusting himself deep inside her pussy, making her convulse again.

Scarlett's moans turn into screams of pleasure. Flipping her back around on her back, Nikolas grabs Scarlett's neck and fucked her harder and faster, getting her to climax faster, fighting the urge to cum deep inside her. She milked his cock as she came. Nikolas pulled out, and before he could cum on her beautiful breasts, Scarlett devoured Nikolas cock deep in her mouth, sucking him deeper and massaging his balls simultaneously. Nikolas' body started to shake as he exploded deep into her mouth. Her hair wrapped around his fingers as he held her still, pumping her lovely mouth with his hot, sticky cum. Nikolas moaned in pleasure, *"Scarlett… Scarlett… Oh fuck Scarlett, I need more of you."* Scarlett looked up, wiping her lips with the tip of her thumb, a smile forming with curiosity. *"How do you need more of me?"* she asked. Nikolas bent down, kissing her passionately. *"I need you in every way possible."* He stared deep into her eyes, falling head over heels in love with her. Scarlett started to fall hard for Nikolas.

Hours later, Scarlett returned to the hospital with a smile that seemed to light up the room. Grandma was reading her book of the month, while Noelle was fast asleep. In that moment, Grandma knew, Scarlett knew that she had found the one, the one who knew how to love in all its forms, two souls finding solace. The future was going to be merry and bright.

Chapter Eighteen

Selfless Act

The next morning, Scarlett hurried down the hospital hallway, her mind consumed with exhaustion and being on cloud nine from her date with Nikolas. After the amazing date they had last night, they kept texting each other. By midmorning, Scarlett had to get something to eat from the hospital café downstairs. But something was nagging at her as if she was forgetting something. Something important, but she couldn't quite put her finger on it.

It was payment day, and the mounting medical bills weighed me down. Lost in her thoughts, Scarlett barely noticed the figure approaching her until she heard a voice calling her name. *"Scarlett, could I have a word with you, please?"*

It was the hospital administrator, her expression grave as she approached her with a stack of papers in hand. Startled, Scarlett nodded, her heart sinking with dread as she realized what this conversation might entail. She followed her to a quiet corner of the hallway, her pulse quickening with each passing moment. "*I'm afraid we need to discuss your outstanding hospital bill,*" the administrator began, her tone business-like yet tinged with sympathy. "*Your daughter's treatments have incurred significant costs, and we need to address the matter of payment.*" Scarlett's stomach churned with anxiety as she listened to the administrator's words, the weight of their financial struggles pressing down on her shoulders like a heavy burden. She knew they were already stretched to their limits, and the thought of not being able to afford Noelle's care filled her with a sense of helplessness.

Just as Scarlett's thoughts began to spiral, a familiar voice cut through the tension like a ray of light. "*Excuse me, but is everything all right here?*" Scarlett turned around with her eyes widened in surprise as she saw Nikolas standing there, his expression one of concern and determination. She hadn't expected him to be here, but at that moment, she felt a surge of gratitude for his presence. The administrator hesitated, taken aback by

Nikolas's sudden appearance. *"Sir, I was just discussing the matter of Scarlett's hospital bill—"* But before the administrator could finish, Nikolas held up a hand, his gaze unwavering as he addressed Scarlett. *"Scarlett, I overheard what was happening. I want you to know that I'm here for you, whatever you need."*

Tears welled up in Scarlett's eyes as she looked at Nikolas, overwhelmed by his kindness and generosity. She hadn't expected him to intervene, but in that moment, she realized just how much he cared for her and Noelle. With a grateful smile, Scarlett nodded, her heart overflowing with emotion. *"Thank you, Nikolas. That means more to me than you'll ever know."* Determined to ease Scarlett's burden, Nikolas turned to the administrator, his voice firm and resolute. *"I'll take care of the hospital bill. Please ensure that Noelle receives the best possible care, no matter the cost."*

The administrator blinked in surprise, clearly taken aback by Nikolas' offer. After a moment of hesitation, she nodded, her expression softening with understanding. *"Of course, sir. We'll make sure that Noelle receives the care she needs.*" As the administrator walked away to finalize the arrangements, Scarlett turned to Nikolas, her eyes shining with gratitude and admiration. In that moment, she realized just how lucky she was to have him by her side, a beacon of hope and support in the darkest of times. With a grateful smile, Scarlett reached out and squeezed Nikolas's hand, silently thanking him for his selfless act of kindness. In that moment, she knew that together, they would face whatever challenges lay ahead.

Walking down the hall, Scarlett held Nikolas' hand. *"Please come upstairs and meet Noelle."* She asked. Nikolas smiled and gave a reassuring squeeze on Scarlett's hand. *"Of course."* He said with a smile. Nikolas stood outside the door of Noelle's hospital room, his heart pounding with anticipation. He knew a great deal about Scarlett's daughter, Noelle, but this would be the first time he would meet her in person as himself and not pretending to be Santa. Taking a deep breath to steady his nerves, he gently pushed open the door and stepped inside.

The room was bathed in soft sunlight streaming in through the window, casting a warm glow over the space. Noelle was lying in her hospital bed, her small frame cocooned in blankets, her face pale but peaceful as she slept. Scarlett sat by her side, her expression a mixture of exhaustion and unwavering love. As Nikolas approached, Scarlett looked up and offered him a weary smile. *"Nikolas, I'm so glad you're here,"* she whispered, her voice filled with gratitude.

Nikolas returned the smile, his gaze shifting to the sleeping figure of Noelle. She looked so fragile, yet there was a strength in her presence that was undeniable. With each steady breath she took, Nikolas felt a surge of admiration for the young girl who was fighting so bravely against her illness. Moving closer to the bed, Nikolas leaned down. He whispered, *"Hey, Noelle. I'm Nikolas. I've heard so much about you, and I'm thrilled to finally meet you."* As he moved a strand of hair out of her face.

Noelle stirred slightly, her eyelids fluttering open to reveal eyes that sparkled with life despite the challenges she faced. She blinked up at Nikolas, her gaze curious yet cautious as she took in his presence. "*Hi,*" she murmured, her voice soft but filled with a hint of curiosity. Nikolas smiled gently, his heart melting at the sight of the brave young girl before him. "*I just wanted to say that I'm here for you, Noelle. Whatever you need, I'm here to support you and your mom.*" Noelle's lips curved into a small smile, a flicker of gratitude shining in her eyes. In that moment, Nikolas knew that he had found a kindred spirit in Noelle, a bond that transcended words and circumstances. And as he stood by her bedside, surrounded by the warmth and love of Scarlett and Noelle, he knew that he was exactly where he was meant to be.

They spent the rest of the day drawing, laughing, and spending time with one another. Nikolas ordered food to be delivered. Noelle's eyes lit up when she saw a cookie milkshake come in. She joyfully asked, "*Is that for me?*" Nikolas chuckled, "Yes, it is, but of course, Mom *makes the final decision.*" Scarlett laughed, "*Only if you eat all of your food.*" Noelle jumped up and danced on her bed with excitement.

As the three of them ate, laughed, and got to know each other, they formed a strong bond. Noelle was excited to announce that *"today was the best day ever, it felt like home."* Nikolas and Scarlett looked at each other and smiled.

Chapter Nineteen

Christmas Eve

The soft morning light filtered through the curtains of Noelle's room, casting a gentle glow over the sterile surroundings. Noelle stirred in her bed, blinking sleepily as she gradually became aware of her surroundings. She glanced at the whiteboard on the wall, and her heart skipped a beat. It was Christmas Eve.

Noelle sat up, the rustle of her blankets echoed in the quiet room, and she couldn't help but feel a pang of sadness at the thought of spending Christmas in the hospital. But then she remembered the promise of the day ahead, a day filled with love, laughter, and the joy of being together with her family.

Noelle's eyes twinkled with excitement as she turned to her mom, who was peacefully sleeping on the chair beside her. Noelle looked at her mom resting, then a cheeky grin came to her face. *"Good morning, Mom! Merry Christmas Eve!"* Startling Scarlett awake, "Good morning, *sweetie, Merry Christmas Eve!"* she says with a great big yawn while stretching her aching back.

Despite the circumstances, she knew that today would be special. Just then, the door to her room creaked open, and Nikolas entered with a bright smile, a small tray in his hands. *"Good morning! Merry Christmas Eve!"* he exclaimed, his voice filled with warmth and love. Noelle's face lit up at the sight of Nikolas, and she couldn't suppress the surge of excitement that bubbled up inside her. *"Merry Christmas Eve, Nikolas!"* she replied, her voice tinged with joy.

Nikolas set the tray down on the bedside table, revealing a festive spread of treats: warm cinnamon rolls, fresh fruit, and a steaming cup of hot cocoa adorned with a candy cane. Noelle's eyes widened in delight at the sight, and she couldn't wait to dig in. As they enjoyed their impromptu Christmas breakfast together, Noelle felt a sense of gratitude wash over her.

Despite the challenges they faced, they were together. A family united by love and resilience. And as she savored each delicious bite, Noelle knew that this would be a Christmas Eve she would never forget.

"Now, should we take the day on by hunting for Santa's reindeer or try to go bobsledding with a yeti?" Nikolas joked with Noelle. *"Can we find Santa's sleigh and go for a ride around the world?"* she replied. Scarlett and Nikolas chuckled at her wild idea. *"Sounds wonderful!"* Nikolas agreed to the crazy idea.

Dr. Smith knocks on the door and enters the room, *"Good morning, Noelle, merry Christmas Eve, how are we doing today?"* Noelle, who is not fond of being reminded that she is stuck in the hospital, said, "Good morning, Merry Christmas Eve, Dr. Smith. *I am well, I say well enough to be discharged to go home as my Christmas present."* Dr. Smith giggled, *"Is that so?"* Dr Smith took his stethoscope and listened to Noelle's chest. *"Mmmhmm,"* Noelle said confidently. Dr. Smith and Nurse Cali sat at the edge of Noelle's bed.

Both Noelle's and Scarlett's hearts sank; the last time they did this was when Noelle got diagnosed with cancer. Time felt frozen. Noelle's eyes became watery as she prepared herself to hear the horrible news. Scarlett was holding Noelle tight, trying to shield her from the bad news the medical team was about to share.

With a heavy sigh, Dr. Smith spoke, "Your recent labs have looked amazing, *Noelle, and Nurse Cali has told me about your expressions about how you want to be home for Christmas. So, you will be discharged today. Merry Christmas, little Noelle. You are going home.*" Noelle and Scarlett both break down in tears, hugging each other.

Nikolas approaches Dr. Smith and shakes his hand. *"Thank you for making today special."* Noelle excitedly exclaims, *"WAIT! Does that mean I get to ring the silver bells?"* she asks. Nurse Cali smiles, "Yes, *sweetie!*" Noelle shoots up out of bed and begins to pack up her belongings. She cannot wait to go home for Christmas.

Scarlett grabs her phone and calls Grandma; she answers the phone, and before anyone could say anything, Noelle screams in excitement, *"Grandma! My Christmas wish came true! I get to go home!"* Grandma, with tears in her eyes, said, "I am on my way, *my little Noelle!*"

A couple of hours later, when the packing is done, the discharge papers are signed. Noelle stood at the entrance of the hospital lobby; her gaze fixed on the towering silver bells that hung above the doorway. Each year, it was tradition for patients who were discharged on Christmas Eve to ring the bells as a symbol of hope and triumph over adversity.

Today, after weeks of treatment and countless days spent in the hospital, it was finally her turn. Her heart fluttered with excitement as she reached out to grasp the gleaming rope that dangled beside the bells. Her fingers wrapped around it, feeling the smooth texture against her skin, and she took a deep breath to steady herself. This moment had been a long time coming, and she couldn't wait to finally ring the bells and step out into the world beyond the hospital walls.

With a determined expression, Noelle pulled down on the rope, feeling the vibrations resonate through her body as the bells began to chime. Their sweet melody filled the air, echoing through the lobby and beyond—a joyful proclamation of victory and resilience. As the last echoes of the bells faded away, a wave of emotion washed over Noelle, Scarlett, Grandma, and Nikolas. Tears filled their eyes as they realized the significance of this moment. The culmination of weeks of hard work, determination, and unwavering support from family and the medical team. Turning to face the crowd gathered behind her, Noelle's eyes sparkled with gratitude as she took in the smiling faces of her loved ones. Her mom, Scarlett, stood beside her. Her eyes were shining with pride and love. As they embraced each other, Noelle knew that she was ready to embark on the next chapter of her journey.

With a final glance at the silver bells, Noelle stepped forward, her heart filled with gratitude and determination. As she walked out into the crisp winter air, she knew that she was not just leaving the hospital behind. She was stepping into the future of being a normal kid.

Upon arriving home, Noelle and Scarlett walked inside their little apartment to find a surprise. Grandma had a feeling that Christmas was going to be extra special this year and decorated the entire apartment. Noelle was thrilled to see all the decorations. Scarlett, Grandma, and Nikolas sat on the couch watching Noelle live the best day ever as she got reunited with everything at home.

That evening, they gathered around in the living room, watching Christmas movies. An exhausted Noelle says between each yawn, *"This is the best Christmas Eve ever."* As she drifts to sleep in her mom's arms. Nikolas picks her up and takes her to bed, tucking her in.

Scarlett starts to have a panic attack as she doesn't have any gifts for Noelle to open on Christmas morning. *"Don't worry, dear, I have been shopping, everything is wrapped and in your closet,"* Grandma mentions. Nikolas chimes in, *"I also have stuff waiting for her as well."* He reaches for Scarlett's hand and gives a reassuring squeeze. *"Thank you to both of you; it has been so hard this year."* She hugs them each.

Nikolas excuses himself and rushes home to get the presents for Noelle that Scarlet had asked for on the Angel tree. But before returning to Scarlett's apartment. Nikolas had to make one last stop.

Chapter Twenty

Forever

As the soft light of dawn filtered through the curtains, Noelle stirred in her bed, her eyes fluttering open to the familiar surroundings of her own room and not the sounds of medical equipment humming. Blinking away the remnants of sleep, she sat up, a smile spreading across her face as she realized that it was Christmas Day.

With a burst of excitement, Noelle jumped out of bed and made her way to the living room. The sound of her footsteps echoes through the quiet apartment. As she reached the living room, her eyes widened in wonder at the sight that greeted her.

The living room was transformed into a winter wonderland, adorned with twinkling lights, garlands of greenery, and a towering Christmas tree that reached towards the ceiling. But it wasn't just the festive decorations that caught her eye. Scattered beneath the tree were piles of brightly wrapped presents, each one adorned with ribbons and bows. Noelle's heart raced with excitement as she realized that they were all for her. With a delighted squeal, she rushed forward, eagerly tearing into the first gift with unbridled enthusiasm. *"Mom! Santa came!"* she called out. Scarlett, Grandma, and Nikolas joined her in the living room. As she unwrapped each present, her eyes lit up with joy at the sight of the treasures hidden within. Books, toys, games, and all the things she had wished for during her time in the hospital.

Meanwhile, Scarlett stood nearby, her heart swelling with happiness at the sight of her daughter's radiant smile. She was thankful for Grandma and Nikolas for preparing this moment, wanting nothing more than to see Noelle happy and healthy on Christmas morning. As she watched Noelle unwrap her gifts with unabashed delight, Scarlett's eyes filled with tears of gratitude. This was the moment she had prayed for.

A moment of pure joy and celebration, a testament to their strength and resilience as a family. Stepping forward, Scarlett wrapped her arms around Noelle, pulling her close in a warm embrace. *"Merry Christmas, sweetheart,"* she whispered, her voice choked with emotion. Noelle looked up at her mom, her eyes shining with happiness. *"Merry Christmas, Mommy."* She replied, her voice filled with love and gratitude.

Scarlett excused herself and walked into the tiny kitchen to make a pot of coffee for everyone. Nikolas stood in the kitchen, his heart pounding with nervous anticipation as he watched Scarlett move about with practiced ease. She hummed softly to herself as she prepared everyone's morning coffee, the rich aroma of freshly ground beans filling the air. Her hair cascaded in soft waves around her shoulders, and the morning sunlight danced across her features, illuminating her beauty in a way that took Nikolas' breath away.

In his hands, he held a small velvet box, its weight a reassuring presence as he rehearsed the words he had been practicing. Today was the day he would ask Scarlett to spend the rest of her life with him, and the thought filled him with a heady mix of excitement and nervousness.

As Scarlett turned to pour the coffee into the mugs, Nikolas took a deep breath, summoning his courage. *"Scarlett,"* he began, his voice wavering slightly with emotion. She turned to face him, a warm smile lighting up her face. *"Yes, Nikolas?"* she asked, her eyes sparkling with curiosity. Nikolas stepped forward, extending the small box towards her with trembling hands. *"I have something for you,"* he said, his voice barely above a whisper. Scarlett's eyes widened in surprise as she accepted the box, her fingers tracing the smooth surface with a mixture of anticipation and excitement. With trembling hands, she lifted the lid, revealing the glimmering ring inside.

Her breath caught in her throat as she held the dazzling diamond ring nestled inside, its brilliance reflecting the love and commitment that Nikolas felt for her. Tears welled up in her eyes as she looked up at him, her heart overflowing with emotion.

"Nikolas, is this...?" she trailed off, her voice choked with emotion. Nikolas nodded, his own eyes glistening with unshed tears. *"Scarlett, I love you more than words can*

describe. Will you do me the honor of becoming my wife?" Silence filled the room as Scarlett stared at him, her heart pounding in her chest. And then, with a radiant smile, she threw her arms around him, pulling him into a tight embrace. *"Yes, Nikolas, yes!"* she exclaimed, her voice filled with joy and love. In that moment, as they stood together in the warm embrace of their kitchen, surrounded by the aroma of coffee and the promise of a future filled with love and happiness, Nikolas knew that he had found the greatest gift of all. The gift of a lifetime spent with the woman he loved more than anything in the world. Nikolas kissed Scarlett tenderly, saving the moment as the woman he fell for was willing to spend forever with him.

Coming back into the living room, beaming from ear to ear. Scarlett announced with Noelle and Grandma that she and Nikolas were engaged to be married. Noelle jumped up from the toy pile and ripped up wrapping paper to give them a hug of approval. Grandma slowly gets up, walks over to the newly engaged couple, and gives her blessing. *"Congratulations to you both. When shall a wedding happen?"* surprised by Grandma's comment, Scarlett cried out, "Mom, *we just got engaged!*" Nikolas had a good belly laugh from it. *"How about New Year's Eve?"* Noelle squeals with excitement, *"YES!"* Speechless from the decision, Scarlett agreed, "New Year's *Eve sounds splendid."*

Several days passed as the hustle and bustle of a New Year's Eve elopement took place. Everything was ready to go.

In a secluded spot, away from the hustle and bustle of the crowds at the park, Scarlett and Nikolas exchanged tender glances, their hearts pounding with anticipation. They made the decision to start the new year as husband and wife, bound together by love and commitment. Beside them stood Grandma, a wise and gentle presence who had been a source of strength and support throughout their journey. And by their side was Noelle, her eyes shining with excitement as she eagerly awaited the momentous occasion.

With a smile, Scarlett and Nikolas turned to face each other, their hands intertwined in a silent promise of forever. In that moment, nothing else mattered but the love they shared and the future they were about to embark upon. As the clock struck midnight on New Year's Eve, Scarlett and Nikolas stood hand in hand beneath a canopy of twinkling stars. The crisp winter air was filled with the distant sound of laughter and music, a joyous cacophony that echoed through the night. As the first fireworks exploded in the sky above, casting a kaleidoscope of colors across the night, Scarlett and Nikolas leaned in to share a tender kiss, whispering into Scarlett's ear, "I love you, *my forever angel."* Scarlett places her hand on Nikolas's cheek. *"I will love you forever."*

Time seemed to stand still as they lost themselves in the sweetness of the moment, the world fading away around them. The final burst of fireworks illuminated the sky in a dazzling display of light and color. Scarlett and Nikolas knew that this was just the beginning of their journey together. With their loved ones by their side and their hearts full of hope, they stepped into the new year hand in hand, ready to face whatever challenges and joys lay ahead, united in love and devotion. The End